First Comes Love

A
Chronicles of Moxie
Novel

Z.B Heller

ISBN: 978-0-9904250-4-5

Dedication

For Lauren

Editor to the stars, teacher to the grammar phobics, and above all else, my friend.
Thank you for helping Moxie grow up and talking me off the ledge…on more then one occasion.

Table of Contents

One

Miles

I wrapped my leg around hers under the sheet and scooped her curvy body close to mine. She was still asleep. Well, from what I could tell, she was. Drool seeping from her mouth was a good indicator. She was restless last night, tossing and turning, mumbling something about a Ferris wheel and churros. I loved this woman. I suspected she still doubted my feelings for her from time to time, but I've told her and tried to show her as much as I could. There was a time when Moxie felt I didn't like the way she looked, that she was too chubby. She couldn't have been more wrong. Granted, I was a guy and, of course, looks were part of a package, but there was something about Moxie's curves that got my dick hard the first time I met her and it hadn't gone fully into flaccid mode since. It must have been her ass, I loved to grip it and smacked it when I walked by. Or maybe it was her boobs. God, Moxie's tits were just…

I would say it was love at first sight, but it was more like confusion at first sight. She was drunk at a bar called Dickie's and had asked me if hairy balls or smooth balls were better. I had thought it was a little early on in our introduction to talk about my manscaping habits, so I tried to answer as diplomatically as I could. Before I could ask her name, she spewed the martinis she had consumed that evening onto my pants and shoes.

It had been a bumpy road for us to get together. I had my son Dillion to consider, and he was my most important priority. Ever since my wife died in a car accident in Maine two years ago, I knew I had to protect my son. He was in the same accident as my wife and had been in a medically induced comma due to the extent of his injuries. A few weeks later, Dillion woke up and I thanked God every day that he was still with me. Since then he's suffered from night terrors and post-traumatic stress. It was a lot for a seven-year-old to handle. Anyone who was going to be in our lives had to understand Dillion had issues and that was part of the package deal. I just never thought it would be his new kindergarten teacher—the same woman who'd hurled on me at the bar.

"Your snake is poking me," Moxie said, her voice raspy with sleep.

"I can't help it. The morning pee alarm is on." I nuzzled my face into her neck. She smelled like the strawberry shower gel she liked to use.

"Never, and I mean never, say the words pee in the bed we have sex in. Is that understood?"

Since Moxie worked with five and six-year-olds at school, the words pee and poo-poo were officially omitted from all our vocabulary. Moxie didn't get the grade change she was hoping for, like working with fifth graders. Instead, Mrs. James, her principal, placed her with first grade because she felt Moxie worked best with the younger kids. That and Moxie admitted she couldn't do math above second grade. To make matters even worse, Moxie had a lot of her students from last year when she taught kindergarten. Even though Moxie liked her principal, she came home one day with a voodoo doll called Mrs. James and stabbed needles in the doll's crotch.

"Sorry, the snake needs to go to the watering hole." I rephrased my statement.

"It's not that much better, although, I wouldn't be surprised if something like that came out of one of my students' mouths."

"Well, maybe after I drain my pipe, the snake would still like to play," I whispered into her ear and nipped her earlobe.

"As much as I would love for you to bury your rattlesnake into my hidey-hole, I have to get up and get ready to go."

"Why are you leaving so early?"

"Because someone in this room, whose name I shall not mention, decided the suburbs would be a great living situation when I have go into the city to work."

"You see that stuff outside?" I pointed to the window. "It's called grass. Little boys need space to spread out and play."

"And what does *Dillion* need?" The corner of her lip twisted up and she raised one eyebrow.

I found her ticklish spot between her hip and ribs and went in for the kill. Another thing I loved about Moxie was her sarcastic, dirty mouth.

"Stop! Truce, I call a truce." She flung herself around the bed to get away from me, finally landing on her stomach with her head in the pillow.

"You're lucky you're cute, and I'll forgive your indiscretions." I whacked her on the ass. "I'll get Dillion up and start some coffee."

Before I left the bed completely, I moved her mane of red hair aside and gave her a kiss on the cheek. She rolled back over and under the covers like a burrito.

"Okay," she whined, her voice muffled under the sheets. "I'll come out never."

I got out of bed and gave my naked body a nice stretch. I usually didn't sleep naked. My boys needed support, even in sleep. But I had been finding it hard to keep any article of clothing on when Moxie slept over. Every time she's around, I felt like a horny teenager and wanted to take her on any surface I could find. I flipped on the bathroom light, wincing at the brightness. I ran my hand over my messy brown hair and then my face, which sported a few days' worth of stubble. Moxie eventually told me she had a thing for brown hair, blue-eyed guys. I, in turn, told her I had a thing for her beautiful red hair and a sweet squeezable ass. Before I met Moxie, I didn't know that was such a turn on for me. But when I saw her at the bar, it was as if my dick had a homing device that pointed straight at her.

I showered, skipped shaving because Moxie liked the scruff, and went back into the bedroom with a towel wrapped around my waist to check on Moxie. She was lucky to have an understanding principal, but her coworker, Amber aka The Wicked Witch of the West, would find a way to use Moxie's tardiness to get her fired.

My gray sheets were gathered into a ball at the bottom of the bed. Damn. I hoped to get an eyeful of naked Moxie when she got up. I supposed the clothed Moxie would have to do.

After dressing, I walked to Dillion's room to rouse him out of bed. His door was open, and I wondered if he was already up. I peeked in and my heart skipped a beat. Moxie was there, already dressed for the day and lying on the twin bed with Dillion. The problem was Moxie was sound asleep, and Dillion was trying to shake her awake.

"I see the morning bird came in to wake you up." I leaned against the doorframe.

Dillion smiled at me. "She tried. I give her an A for effort but F for execution."

That was my son, the fifty-year-old in a seven-year-old body. Even in my thirties, Dillion surpassed my intelligence, and I wasn't exactly stupid. He probably surpassed me in the maturity department, too. But I would never fess up to that in public. Dillion did take after me in the looks department. He shared my blue eyes and brown hair, except he was able to pull off the cute shaggy hair like a sheepdog. If I tried that, I would look like a dipshit.

"You have my permission to sit on her head until she stops breathing." I winked at him.

"Daaaad," Dillion moaned.

"Fine. Shake her awake and get ready. Don't forget to brush your teeth. No one wants to smell your breath when it stinks like an elephant's butt." Dillion looked down at Moxie again and giggled before he climbed over her sleepy body to get out of bed.

I walked into the kitchen and flipped the switch on the coffee maker. I took two mugs out of the cabinet. Moxie's favorite mug said, "If you value your life, don't speak to me until this is done." That was one of the things Moxie and I had in common. Our day didn't officially begin until caffeine rotted away our arteries. My cell phone beeped with an incoming text. I grabbed it off the counter.

Yo, douche. Want to catch some brews after work?

It was Jeff Camden. He worked with me at the station. I was a graphic designer for the television station and he was in production. We managed to become friends, though, I wasn't exactly sure how, considering he was an asshole most of the time, but he was nice to me when we moved here and I didn't know a soul besides my sister Kelly. As cool as Kelly was, she didn't have enough testosterone to talk about blow jobs. Not that I went around talking about blow jobs to random people, but it was nice to know there was a guy I could converse about it if needed.

Kelly is taking Dillion out to the museum, so I'm going to surprise Moxie at school.

I hit send and went to the refrigerator to get cream for my coffee while I waited for what I was sure was going to be some insightful words from Jeff.

Dude, your penis is going to shrivel and die from overuse. You gotta let it breathe once in a while. Like fine wine.

And I was right. He was so predictable.

You wouldn't know the first thing about fine wine, considering you thought Perrier was a type of Chardonnay.

You think I pay attention to that shit, asshole? I just let the lady order what she likes because it gives me better access to her bush.

I groaned and rolled my eyes before responding.

Don't say bush.

Why?

Because a pussy isn't a fucking shrub.

I ran my hand down my face while I shook my head.

Dude, I went out with this Russian chick. You should

have seen what I was dealing with. I needed a pair of hedge trimmers just to find the hole.

See you at work, Jeff.

I hadn't had enough coffee yet to deal with Jeff.

"Why did Dillion say that you had a death wish for me?" Moxie strolled into the kitchen with her hair pulled in a ponytail. All I could think of as I watched her hair swish back and forth over her bare neck was how I wanted to pull on it while working her from behind.

My sexually charged thoughts cleared when my son tagged behind Moxie. I gave him the stink eye, but feigned innocence when I said to Moxie, "What are you talking about?"

"Something about smothering me in my sleep." She nailed me down with a glare. A glare she would give her students. But she wasn't going to school me. She looked at me as if I were one of her students in trouble.

"Oh, he misunderstood. I meant tap her gently and sing softly until she rises." I laughed, crossing my arms over my chest.

She walked up to me, grabbed my junk, and pulled. I let out an oomph and gripped the counter. Thankfully, Dillion was in the pantry, digging out some breakfast. She gave my dick a delicate caress, and I couldn't help reacting to her touch. I grew hard because in truth, I was a guy and if Moxie touched my penis, it was going to respond. I would need to collect myself before going into work. I didn't want to scare my coworkers by walking around with a hard-on. Except for Ryan. I'm sure he'd love to get an eyeful of what I sported in my jeans. Ryan liked to tease me that one day he was going to get me to play for the same team. I told him that if I ever changed my mind and suddenly liked dick, he would be the first in line to win my affection.

"Next time when you disturb my slumber, I will detach this, make a mold of it, and use it for my pleasure. Then I won't have to deal with the rest of you."

"Can you at least ask them to put on another three inches to the mold? I always felt that I lacked in the length department." I wiggled my eyebrows.

She let go and pressed her lips onto mine. She tasted minty.

"Miles, if your dick was any longer, it would go in my pussy and come out my throat," she said as she stepped back and winked.

Not going to lie, that was so fucking hot. It was nice to have my ego stroked, especially when it had to do with my manhood.

I grabbed her hips and pulled her back. Her breasts pushed against my chest, making my manhood even more rock hard. I pressed my forehead against hers and then kissed her full lips. After a moment, I pulled back because if I continued, I wouldn't be able to stop. Moxie had the power to take over my brain, and I could lose myself in her for hours. Some people might call me pussy whipped, but I didn't fucking care.

"What are you doing after school?" I asked while she gathered her things for school in her bag. I poured myself a cup of coffee and changed Moxie's cup to a tumbler she could take with her.

"Besides stringing Katie the Girl Scout Savage by the toes, I was thinking of going to Dickie's with Renee."

"Planning on taking any interesting bar polls this evening?" I leaned against the counter and flashed her my most devilish smile. Dickie's was the bar where we first met when she asked me if I preferred hairy balls to smooth balls.

"Yes. Tonight's question might have to do with the topic of nipple hair. To shave or not to shave." Acting as if she were really contemplating the question, she looked to the ceiling while scratching her chin.

All I could do was shake my head at my little spitfire. "Well, try to keep the contents of your stomach to yourself."

"No worries. I only give you the vomit treatment. It's kind of like a dog marking its territory. So you should have been honored when I lost the contents of my stomach on you the first time we met."

"Dad, can I have Frosted Flakes for breakfast?" Dillion skipped over to us with the box.

"I never bought Frosted Flakes," I said, grabbing the box in confusion. I tried to steer Dillion away from sugary cereal in the morning.

"Oh geez, look at the time." Moxie looked at her watch. She snatched her keys from the counter, grabbed the box of cereal, and kissed both Dillion and I on the cheeks. "Gotta go! Don't want to be late for hell… I mean school."

There went my beautiful redhead, leaving a trail of flames everywhere she went. I couldn't help but laugh because even though she would do sneaky things, there was no way I could douse those flames.

Two

Moxie

I needed to stay late after school to prepare for teacher conferences. I hated conferences, especially for first grade. How do you tell a parent their child was doing great in math when they couldn't even button their own pants. Most of the time it was a chore, keeping their own snot from becoming an afternoon snack. It was as if I worked in a nursing home, making sure everyone's tushies were wiped and making sure no one played doctor in the closet. Well, in that one case, behind the puppet show area. I thought I would leave that all behind when I left kindergarten. But apparently first grade was like kindergarten except the kids were three inches taller.

Luckily for me not many of my fellow teachers stayed

after school that day, so things were nice and quiet for optimal concentration. Which was complete bullshit as I would be here all night if I didn't detach myself from the entertainment gossip websites. Reading about Taylor Swift's umpteenth breakup was much more exciting than documenting who was not getting along in class.

There was a knock on the door. I looked up and Miles stood there, looking better then Matt Bomer and Channing Tatum put together. My man was handsome, the handsomest guy on earth. But I'm not bias or anything.

"Hey there." I tried to roll my tongue back into my mouth.

"Hey there, yourself." He strode toward my desk, his hands in the pockets of his ass hugging jeans. *My* favorite ass hugging jeans. I had to remember to ask where he'd gotten those jeans so I could buy out the entire store.

"If you're here to pick up Dillion, you may have forgotten that you stole him from me. He is in this weird play called"—I used air quotes—"The Suburbs. It's a mythical place full of minivans and soccer fields." I loved giving Miles a hard time for living in the burbs.

"He's with Kelly. I had to work a little longer than normal, and since it's Friday, she volunteered to take him to the Museum of Science and Industry. Dillion has a thing about watching the baby chicks hatch from their eggs."

"Well, he is a very nurturing child. Better be careful or you're going to end up with a coop filled with chickens in your backyard." I imagined Dillion going out each morning to check on his chickens in his industrialized coop. "So you're done working and you decide to spend quality quiet time at an elementary school?"

"Maybe I have a crush on the teacher, and I wanted to see if I could get extra credit," he said in a seductive tone.

I knew that tone very well. It was the tone of heat, lust, and pure sex. Miles bent over my desk, resting his hands on top. He had rolled up his shirtsleeves, giving me a wonderful glimpse of his large forearms. I wanted to take my tongue and run it up and down his strong arms. God, I wished I were behind him so I could enjoy the view from the back. Although, I certainly wouldn't complain about the view from the front either.

"I need to work on these conference reviews or else I'm going to have to tell all the parents that their children's favorite part of the day is lunch and recess."

The corner of his mouth went up. "Well, it is."

"Of course it is, but I have to make the parents believe I'm teaching the next Albert Einstein. Unfortunately, I don't have a student like Dillion anymore to teach the class for me while I stalk Facebook and eat Reese's Peanut Butter Cups all day."

Dillion had joined my class toward the end of the school year after he and Miles moved from Maine last year. Needless to say I was completely shocked when I found out that his dad was the same person I had upchucked on the weekend before.

"Don't tell him that. He might take you up on it and start

spouting Hemingway to the class."

"Who's Hemingway?" I smiled and put my thumb and forefinger to my chin thoughtfully and looked to the ceiling

"Don't let Dillion hear you say that. He'll tell you all about the book *The Old Man and the Sea* until you know Hemingway better than Hemingway did."

I couldn't contain my laughter. I could see Dillion in front of the class like a little college professor, in his tweed coat and smoking a pipe, lecturing the life and times of good old Ernst. Dillion was certainly a special child—no question there. I couldn't help but feel protective of him from other kids. He had a hard time connecting to other students because of his intellectual level, and I feared he would become the target of bullies. If that were ever to happen, I would sit on the bullies and suffocate them with my lovely ass.

"Dillion has a unique way about him. Has he always been like that?" I asked, hoping I could distract him from giving me that look that said, "I want to fuck you now."

"Yup. He just has an old soul. I think he gets it from my dad."

"You're not exactly dumb yourself, you know. I mean, you're dating me and that makes you a genius in my book."

"Thank you. You know if you're not careful with that smartass mouth of yours, I'll have to teach it a lesson." He crossed his arms over his broad chest.

My plans for distraction went out the window when his pectorals and forearms flexed. I was never going to get anything accomplished if I looked at the man meat in front of me. It was as if someone was holding a raw piece of steak in front of a hungry lioness. I wanted to attack, but held myself back. I didn't want to throw myself at Miles every time he looked at me that way.

"I thought I was the teacher here," I whispered, standing from my chair and leaning over my desk.

Miles walked slowly over to my side of the desk, playing the role of the lion seeking his mate. There was fire in his eyes and my thighs tightened instantly, trying to relieve the pressure building in my lady garden. He tilted my chin up and looked directly into my eyes.

"You might be the school teacher, but I'm a sex educator and you have gotten in trouble in my class." His voice was low and deep.

My heart pounded and all the blood flow went straight into my groin. "So what is the punishment, professor? Should I write: I've been a bad girl, over and over on the chalkboard?"

Miles cleared everything off my desk with one swipe of his arm, sending everything crashing to the floor. That was going to be a bitch to clean up later, but I didn't care; I was so damned turned on.

"To start your punishment you will have to have to come here." He stood up and pointed to the spot in front of him.

We were face-to-face, our chests grazing. My nipples tightened into tiny stones, aching to be soothed. Miles towered over me, so I had to look at him to say something, but before I could come up with a snarky reply, he spun me around to face the desk. His front pressed hard against my back. He kissed the back of my neck, and the feeling sent shivers through my body.

"You know what I do to students who smart-mouth me?" His warm breath tickled my ear. I pressed my backside into his crotch. I was already needy and impatient.

"Professor, do you get a lot of women mouthing off to you when you teach? I mean some of your teachings are wrong and I feel it's my civil duty to correct you." I enjoyed this game, and I could tell he did too from the stiff boner poking my ass.

"Really? Do tell me what I'm doing wrong." He rubbed his hands up and down my arms, kissing my neck from my ear down my shoulder. My concentration was waning, but I wouldn't give him the satisfaction of breaking me down first.

"The lecture on oral sex sucked," I said.

"That's kind of the point." He bit my shoulder and squeezed my ass. I let out a groan. "I think your punishment is going to have to include this and my very large hand." He continued to rub my ass gently until he gave me a good whack on my backside. That just turned me on even more. Not that I was interested in floggers and riding crops, but a nice spanking was always a fun distraction. His hands slipped around to the front of my jeans and undid the top button.

"Miles, we are in my classroom and the janitor can walk in at any moment," I half moaned, half cried.

"If you're as wet as I think you are, they are going to have an interesting time mopping that off the floor."

I had to admit, I loved that Miles was a dirty talker during sex. He was right; I was probably wet as a lagoon at Sea World. Miles unzipped my jeans and pulled them down my thighs. He ran his hands up my back and bent me forward so my cheek was against the bare desktop. Miles hooked his fingers into the top of my panties and pulled them down to meet my jeans. I felt the cool air in the room hit my most sensitive spot and I started to pant.

"Mmm, I like you this way, bent over to do whatever I want with."

"And what would those plans be?" I asked, barely able to speak.

Miles didn't answer. Instead he sank to his knee and spread my legs as far apart as he could since my jeans were wrapped around my ankles. His finger gently swept across my sex, and I thought I would pass out. That would have been embarrassing, explaining to Mrs. James why I was in a heap on the floor with my pants around my ankles.

"I was right. Nice and wet," he said, stroking me inside and out.

"I couldn't help it; my new professor got me worked up."

"Lucky bastard," he said as he took me his time devouring me, his lips and tongue doing wonders.

"Oh God!" I clutched the edge of the desk. He worked his magical tongue and fingers in a perfect rhythm. He swirled, flicked, and lavished every part of my pussy, making me go insane.

"Miles, I'm going to come!" I huffed, but it didn't even slow him down. Heat gathered in my stomach and poured into my groin. I exploded around his fingers and his mouth, barely able to call his name. As I was coming down from the high of my orgasm, Miles stood and undid his own zipper of his pants.

"Moxie, I need to be inside of you, now," he said through his teeth.

I was still dazed from my own release, and couldn't answer him.

He positioned himself at my at my entrance and slowly filled me, grabbing my hips when he settled in the whole way. He rocked back and forth, shoving me against my desk with each thrust. I whimpered as he started moving faster.

"More. Faster!" I demanded.

He followed my plea as he pumped into me faster and harder. He bent over my, melding my body with his. He whispered in my ear, "Fuck, Moxie! You feel amazing. I can't get enough of you. Come for me, baby. Give me one more."

As soon as the words left his mouth, I screamed in pleasure. But Miles covered my mouth, trying to drown out the noise so we wouldn't attract unwelcome guests. He buried his head between my neck and shoulder, and I felt him squeeze his eyes and mouth shut as his own release followed mine.

We were both sweaty and sticky but couldn't care less. Miles peeled himself off me and helped me stand from the desk. He wrapped his big arms around me.

"Punishment delivered."

"Thank you, sir. May I have another?" I turned around in his arms and placed my hands around his neck.

"You, my little student, can have as much as you want." He gave me a deep kiss that made my toes curl.

He relaxed his hold on me and lifted my underwear and jeans back up. He pressed a soft kiss by my belly button before redressing himself as well.

"You really know how to work up a girl's appetite. I'm starving."

"Sorry, I just ate." He flashed me a devilish grin.

"Gross!" I slapped his chest, laughing at his crass joke.

"Let me take you out. How about Chinese food?"

"Wow. Good sex and Chinese food? I really struck gold with you, didn't I?"

"I aim to please."

"Well, you aimed and hit a bull's-eye. Let's go to LuLu's. They have amazing dumplings."

"They can't be better then your dumplings," he said, pointing at my chest.

I rolled my eyes and grabbed my bag. "Come on, stud muffin. Let's go before I eat your dumpling." I pointed to his crotch.

"Promise?" he replied with a wink.

We worked together to put the items Miles brushed off my desk back into place. I packed my bag and turned off the classroom light as we walked out of door, hand-in-hand.

Three

Moxie

I decided to have an impromptu triple date at LuLu's and called Renee and Ryan to bring their significant others, Raj and Tom. It was great knowing we'd created this little family with our friends. Miles called Kelly on the way to the restaurant to check in and see how Dillion's museum adventure had gone. He then promised Dillion to spend all of Saturday together doing whatever he wanted since Miles had to work late tonight.

It made my heart swell knowing Miles was such a loving and involved father. He also informed Kelly that if she needed Miles to come home earlier he could be there in a flash. Before I knew of Dillion's PTSD months ago, Miles used to disappear every time his sister called when Dillion had panic attacks. I thought Miles was already involved when he ran off on a moment's notice without explanation.

After Miles had explained the whole situation to me, and I'd seen Dillion's night terrors first hand, I wanted to run back with Miles so I could comfort Dillion, too. However, I didn't think we were at the substitute-Moxie-for-deceased-mom phase in our relationship yet.

Everyone was supposed to meet at LuLu's at seven. I was so hungry from playing good teacher, bad student with Miles earlier that even the koi in the makeshift pond at the restaurant looked good. Renee and Raj arrived first. Renee was one of my best friends. We met when I started teaching my first year at the same school. She taught fifth grade and at the time, I taught kindergarten. Quickly, Renee became my confidant and enabler of all things chocolate, and since I was an only child, she became my honorary sister.

"Hey, douchebag," Renee said and came in for a hug.

"Hey, slut face," I retorted as I squeezed her back.

Renee and I always had an interesting friendship. To others, our terms of endearments would be interpreted as insults. But if anyone who knew us heard us refer to the other as *sweetheart* or *honey*, then they knew we were pissed off and wished bodily harm on one another. I was not sure what I would do without Renee as my wingman, but I knew I was lucky enough to have her. She even pretended once to be my lesbian lover when we ran into a clingy one-night stand of mine. She had grabbed me and stuck her tongue down my throat right in front of him. Renee was the only woman I would ever let do that.

Tom came through the door next. "I'm just asking you to put your dishes in the dishwasher when you're done using them. I know your hands and arms work."

"You weren't exactly complaining about my hands and arms this morning when I jacked you off in the shower," Ryan replied.

Tom turned bright red before he greeted us. I rolled my eyes at Ryan. "How do you put up with his shit, Tom?" I asked.

"Because I'm a terrific lay, and I put up with his bullshit OCD ways," Ryan answered for him.

Ryan was my other best friend. We had met at a New Year's Eve party years ago when I was hammered and shamelessly came on to him. Ryan crushed my hopes and dreams that night when he revealed he was gay. I should have guessed he was batting for the other team by how impeccably dressed he was, but I never liked to assume. You know, because when you assume, you make an *ass* out of *U* and *me*. However, in that case I just made a huge ass out of myself. I had woken up the next morning and found Ryan asleep on my couch. Being the gentleman he was, he had made sure I got home safe and nursed my hangover from hell.

Tom was Ryan's boyfriend and, while I thought he was a sweet guy, I didn't know if they made the right pair. Tom was very straitlaced and obsessive about everything from salad fork placement on the table to using Seventh Generation dish detergent instead of Dawn. Ryan was much more laid-back and forgot to put the toilet seat down ninety-nine percent of the time. I found this out once when I crashed at their place and had to pee in the middle of the night. Three words: surprise ass bath.

"Okay," I said. "While this is all mushy and cute, if I don't eat something now, I'm going to have to cannibalize one of you."

"Go for Ryan first," Renee said. "He's got the most muscle on him."

I chuckled as the hostess led us to our table. We all took our menus and silently looked them over. I became uncomfortable because I didn't know if Miles was into the whole sharing a dish thing. It seemed somewhat intimate to share Chinese food. I've only shared dishes with Renee and Ryan because they were my best friends and I felt comfortable ordering family style with them. Although he did have his penis inside of me earlier and things probably couldn't have been more intimate than that, in my mind, sharing Chinese was like proposing marriage.

"What are you getting?" Miles leaned into me and looked at my menu as if it were different than his own.

"Umm, I like the chicken fried rice, but their prawns and broccoli sounds good, too. But they have good lo mein, as well."

"Let's get the prawns and friend rice." He snapped his menu shut.

I looked at him, wide-eyed.

"What?" he asked.

"You're sharing your food with me."

"I can order something else if you want those things for yourself." He opened his menu back up.

"No!" I responded quickly. "It's just no one I was dating has ever shared their Chinese with me."

"I guess you haven't learned that I'm not everyone." He winked

Crap, there went my panties. They burst into flames when Miles talked to me like that. I'm going to have to keep an open account at Victoria's Secret from the way I went through undergarments. I'd never dated anyone like Miles before. Well, truth be told I never really dated. Sure there were occasional hook ups that maybe lasted a week or so, but never something as serious as my relationship with Miles. No one before him ever made me feel comfortable in my own skin.

"Are you ready for conferences?" Renee turned toward me after the waiter took her order.

"Well, I was on a roll until someone plowed me down." I smirked and looked at Miles, who was chatting with Ryan.

"At work? You had sex at work?" Renee squeaked.

"Shh! Why don't you just tell the whole restaurant?"

"Moxie, chances are that eighty percent of this restaurant has already seen your coochie, so I don't think any of this would be a surprise." She smirked.

"Excuse me, but that blind man in the corner has not seen any of my jiggly bits. The rest of the restaurant, I can't speak for."

"I will speak for the other eight percent and say that her jiggly bits are amazing," Miles said, cutting into the conversation.

We were all about to dive into our appetizers when a nice-looking couple approached us.

"Tom?" asked the mystery man.

Everyone at the table stopped talking and looked at Tom, whose face turned the same shade of white as the steamed rice.

"John. Umm, what are you doing here?" Small beads of sweat started forming on Tom's forehead. I watched Ryan for his reaction to this development.

"I'm here with my friend Liv having dinner because you told me you were going to see your mom in the hospital."

Oh shit. I didn't like where this was headed. It was like watching a horror movie and waiting for something or someone to jump out with a hatchet or some crazy shit like that. We were waiting for the hatchet.

"Well, Tom would have had to travel quite a distance to see his mother. Like six feet underground." Ryan's eyes burned holes into Tom's head so hard, I expected his skull to burst into flames.

"Who is this prissy fairy?" The mystery man pointed his finger to Ryan.

Oh, double Dutch chocolate shit. It was about to get ugly.

"This fairy is his boyfriend," Ryan announced as he passively placed his arm around Tom's shoulder. "And who are you besides this woman's little bitch?"

Tom sat there with his mouth hanging open, his eyes bouncing back and forth between the two men like a tennis match.

Mystery man grunted. "Well, boyfriend, you might want to know that your so-called other half had his dick lodged up my—"

"Okay!" Miles held his hand in the air to stop mystery man from finishing his sentence.

Ryan turned to Tom. "What the fuck is this all about?"

My own anger rose and I decided Tom had better cough up some answers before I created a new dish on the menu called Tom's Peking Dick.

"Honey, I can explain." Tom's voice shook.

"Oh, this should be good." I groaned and Miles gave me a little nudge under the table.

"Is there somewhere we can go talk?" Tom took Ryan's chin between his fingers, trying desperately to gain his attention.

"Yeah, maybe you two can go to my apartment where your boyfriend sucked on my—"

I stood up from the table, my chair falling backward and

startling mystery man and the rest of the diners. "Listen, fuck twat. Say one more word and I'll stick this pupu platter up your *poo-poo* so you'll never be able to poo again in your life."

"Who's this bitch?" Mystery man waved his hand in my direction.

"She's my bitch!" Renee stood up. Miles sat back in his chair with his arms folded across his chest and a smirk on his lips. Knowing him, watching me get all fired up turned him on. I expected some explosive sex later.

"And who the fuck are you?" mystery man asked as he looked at Renee.

That's when Ryan got out of his seat. "Those, you motherfucker, are my best friends."

"Ryan, please," Tom begged, pulling on his arm. "Let's go somewhere and talk."

"What?" mystery man piped in. "You can't defend yourself? You have to have someone with a pussy do it for you? No wonder Tom went looking for a real dick when all he had was pussy at home."

"Miles?" I looked down at my boyfriend as I took fighting position.

"Yes?" He looked up. Miles wasn't phased by all the drama. After dating me for a while, he figured out there was always something crazy happening around me.

"If something happens to me, make sure you clear the hard drive on my computer. I'm donating my porn collection to you."

"Even the woman with three tits?" He chuckled.

"No. Make sure I'm buried with that one."

"Damn." He pounded the table with his fist. "I thought for sure that one was mine."

Renee and I moved around the table to stand in front of the douchebag. His shoulders shook with his laughter. Did we amuse him?

"What are you girls going to do? Claw me to death with your Lee Press On Nails?"

Miles tsk-tsked behind me. He knew what was in store for the bastard who hurt one of my best friends.

"I'll put ten dollars down that Renee will land the final blow," Raj said to Miles.

"I'll take your ten and raise you another twenty that Moxie will make sure he's permanently blind afterward," Miles responded.

However, they were both proven wrong when Ryan barreled toward mystery man and tackled him onto the table next to ours. Plates, silverware, and glasses went crashing and people jumped out of the way. Ryan wrestled the asshole while Renee and I watched in amazement. Ryan was strong, but I never realized he had the drive to take on another man and beat his ass down.

Liv, the petite woman with mystery man, pounced onto

Ryan's back. No way was I about to let that happen. I quickly looked around the room. I wanted to make a statement, and that bitch was going to get knocked the fuck out, but I didn't want to get my new top bloody.

Without thinking—as usual—I ran to the front of the restaurant and stuck my hand in the koi pond.

"What you doing? What you doing? No fish, no fish!" The little Chinese hostess ran behind me, hoping to save the koi I had chosen as my club.

"This is what your crotch smells like!" I whacked the girl clawing Ryan's back.

She hopped off Ryan and faced me. She wrinkled her nose and tried swatting the fish out of my hand. "Are you really hitting me with a fish?"

Renee approached, holding a pair of chopsticks like little machetes. "What the fuck are you doing?" I asked her.

"What? You're allowed to use a fish, and I can't use chopsticks? That seems a little unfair."

"But I'm Wonder Woman in this fight and you're whoever Wonder Woman's sidekick is."

"Are you kidding me? I don't want to be a fucking sidekick. My chopsticks are small but mighty. I can poke someone's eye out." Renee waved her chopsticks in the air.

The next thing I knew, a fist hit my face, and I stumbled back into someone's table and into their chicken lo mein.

"That's a waste of good Chinese food," I managed to say.

A pair of large hands took my arms and helped me up from the noodle pool I was sitting in. I looked over Miles's shoulder at the crotch monster I had miserably failed to take down.

Miles bent down and lifted me over his shoulder, giving me a perfect view of his ass. As Miles walked toward the door, I lifted my head, raised a fist, and called out to the people in the restaurant, "The Fish Ninja will return, just you wait!"

Four

Miles

Ten days had passed since, what I liked to refer to as Koi Gate, had happened. Moxie sported the yellow-brown remnants of a nasty black eye from the bitch who'd punched her in the face. The bruise wasn't as bad as the restaurant bill we had to pay for the koi fish Moxie murdered trying to protect Ryan's honor. Koi aren't cheap. I told her I thought it was sexy when she tried to be all gallant even if she smelled of giant goldfish. She didn't appreciate my humor and threatened to stick another one of the koi up my ass. She was so hot when she was feisty.

There was something else bothering Moxie following the incident at the restaurant. I kept asking her what was wrong, but she just gave me the *everything is fine* answer. I'd been around women long enough to know that was code for *something is totally wrong, but you have to become a clairvoyant and figure it out for yourself.* But I was a man and I'd been told that our species was obtuse. Or at least that was what the *Men Are From Mars, Women Are From Venus* book said, or something to that effect. I figured I would wait it out, and when she was ready to talk to me, I'd be here. I might have to wear a cup to protect the family jewels, but I would be willing to listen.

Moxie's holiday break from school was coming up, and I had a massive plan in place for it. She was overdue for a vacation, and what I had planned would make it a vacation she would never forget. But I needed help setting everything into motion, The perfect person for the job was Ryan, but he was still distressed. Tom had been cheating on him with several different guys over the past six months, so Ryan kicked him out. Because Tom was so OCD, he'd been able to cover his tracks, leaving Ryan in the dark. After everything went down, Ryan went into a huge depression, eating Ben & Jerry's and binge watching *Project Runway*. Moxie went over there to his place a few times, but wasn't able to make it past the door even after threatening to burn his favorite Marc Jacobs V-neck sweater. But I needed Ryan's help if I was going to make this plan work. I picked up my phone and send him a text.

> *Hey man, how are you?*

I waited awhile before I finally got a response.

> *If you are someone with a penis, I no longer speak to your breed.*

Don't you think it's time to rejoin society?

Don't you think it's time you become gay and sucked my dick?

This was going to be harder then I thought.

I need yours and Renee's help.

Her birthday isn't until May, dude.

Whose? Renee?

No, Moxie's, dipshit.

I swore if I didn't feel bad for him, I'd go to his place and throttle him. However, I was trying to be patient about Ryan's heartbreak. Moxie said we would give him ten more days to mope and then we were taking him to a gay bar to get laid. I corrected her and told her that *she* would be taking him to a gay bar to get laid.

I know that, asswipe. That's not what I need help with.

Man, I know you think I am the sex king, however, I couldn't tell you what to do with a vagina.

I need your advice about vaginas as much as I need advice on how to lick my own balls.

Moxie doesn't do that for you?

Listen, dickhead, are you going to help or not?

Fuck, man. No need to jump down my throat. I only

reserve that for guys I'm screwing.

I need to get Moxie out of here. She needs a vacation. She seems out of sorts, and I thought a getaway might be good for her.

That and I wanted to keep all of our sanities intact. Her mood swings lately were making my head spin.

And how does this involve me?

It involves you, Renee, and Dillion.

If you're asking me to go to Wisconsin Dells, there is no fucking way it's going to happen.

I was thinking more like Disney World.

Are you fucking Goofy?

Just think about it, okay? Crap, Moxie's here, gotta run.

Sure, just leave me to rot and plan my days as a single man with four hundred cats.

Moxie walked into the room just as I was about to lecture Ryan about being too dramatic and the proper usage of puns. I made sure to delete the texts. If everything fell into place, this vacation would be the best of her life. The most complicated part of this plan was telling Moxie I wouldn't be going with her.

"Hey, sweetness," I said as I approached her. She held her hands to stop me from getting closer. Her face had a greenish tint. "What's wrong? You don't look so hot."

She narrowed her blue eyes and actually bared her teeth like a rabid dog. "Are you saying that I'm not hot anymore?" she hissed. "'Cause let me tell you, that whole nose hair trimming thing you've got going on makes me what to shove daggers in my eyes."

Whoa, that came out of left field. Okay, I admitted my nose hair wasn't the most appetizing thing to watch. But why the hell was she watching? That was kind of creepy.

"And since we're on the subject of things that aren't hot, let's talk about the moaning sound you make when you chew your food. It's like your fucking the food you eat."

"Funny, I could have sworn you like that moaning sound I make when I eat *you*." I smirked. Yes, I knew I was provoking her, but a pissed off Moxie was a sexy Moxie. Instead of the conversation turning into hot foreplay, she pushed against my chest and walked to the bedroom, mumbling under her breath. When she slammed the door, the whole house shook. From my experience over the years, I learned women were complicated and when to pick my battles. But I was not to let her walk all over me. My mother taught me to always respect someone, even if they were acting like a raving maniac on crack.

Shortly after Moxie's grand entrance and disappearance, Dillion came home from school. I was happy my son was home because he always seemed to calm Moxie down. And if that didn't work, I could always use him as a deflector if Moxie started throwing things at me.

"Hey, Dad." My son dropped his backpack on the kitchen chair.

I rubbed his floppy brown hair and gave him a hug. "Hey, dude. How was your day?"

"It was okay. I told Mrs. Richards that my dad's girlfriend is also a teacher."

"Oh yeah? Did she think that was cool?"

"Yes, until I told her that Moxie said the youth of today were headed for an eternity in hell."

Moxie flew out of the bedroom like a bat out of hell, nostrils flaring, eyes thinned to slits. She had my nose trimmer in her hand.

"See!" she shouted. "It's got little hairs that used to be in your nose stuck in it. How would you feel if I put these little nose hairs in your teeth?"

It was then she noticed Dillion, and as if the little man was a salve, Moxie's tense shoulders dropped and her features softened.

"Hey, kiddo," she said while she hid the trimmer behind her back.

"Trying to get that one hair on your chin again?" Dillion asked, putting a finger on his chin.

I raised my eyebrows at Moxie. My son had some balls; I was so proud. I was still confused by Moxie's tirade. I could do the asshole guy thing and blame it on her time of the month, but that time usually resulted in Moxie lying on the floor, screaming that she thought she was dying.

"I may or may not have used this trimmer to remove the goat hairs that reside on my chin," she said, straightening her shoulders and putting the trimmer on the counter. Dillion giggled, grabbed a snack from the fridge, and walked into the other room to use his tablet.

"I call truce," I said, walking up to her and putting my arms around her waist. I kissed her forehead. She sunk into my arms and reciprocated my hug. "What happened? Talk to me."

"I'm sorry," she said. "I don't know why, but everything seems to send me over the edge these days. Mrs. Walker, the lunch lady, said that they were out of tater tots at lunch today, and I threatened to tie her up by her hairnet and dip her in hot oil."

Suddenly, I became fearful of my life. If Moxie was sent over the edge by the lunch lady, whom she worshiped, then anything I said could send her over the edge. I had to tread carefully.

"Guess what? I have a surprise!" I pushed Moxie's shoulder back so I could look at her face. I plastered on a fake smile and started to bounce on my feet. "I booked a vacation to Disney World for winter break."

The room was silent for two beats, and then Dillion screamed with excitement and ran all over the house as if his pants were on fire. He'd been asking me to take him to Disney forever, and this will make it a vacation he hopefully will never forget.

"Umm, wow. This is kind of sudden. You didn't think to ask me about this first?" Moxie didn't radiate the same excitement Dillion had.

I tried to gage her reaction. She bit the corner of her lip and her forehead formed a crease. "I figured you were stressed and could use a little break from the daily grind. I wanted it to be a surprise." I rubbed her shoulders. Her reaction wasn't what I had hoped for. Instead of being excited at the prospect of a vacation, Moxie looked as if she were a million miles away.

Finally breaking out of her trance, she said, "You're right. It will nice to get out of here for a little while. The three of us haven't gone away together since that time at Lake Geneva in the summer."

I held my breath and rub her shoulders to ease some of the stress I felt gathering in her muscles.

"There's a small problem in the plan." The words were almost painful to hear.

"What? Is Martha coming? Because she could easily be counted as one of the Disney villains." Moxie smiled.

"No, Martha isn't going. But if you want her to—"

"No!"

That wasn't a surprise. Moxie hated her stepmother. I inhaled deeply and looked toward the ceiling, praying for some help from mystical powers. "I'm not going," I finally choked out.

"What?" The shrill sound of her voice made the windows around the room crack. She turned around to face me, daggers shooting from her eyes and heading right at me.

"I need to stay here for work. They won't let me take any time off. I even tried begging. But I thought it would be good for you to get away. I even invited Ryan and Renee to go." I pumped my fists in the air. "Yay, group trip!"

When I got cold silence, I went on. "It's going to be so fun, and it's an awesome way for you and Dillion to bond."

But there was nothing but silence and eye daggers. *Shit!* I knew she would be pissed, but I was going through this whole ruse for us and we would look back on it and say, "Remember that time you almost castrated me with a hair trimmer?"

Moxie turned to the counter and picked up the hair trimmer. She looked at me with a mix of sadness and anger and then turned around to walk back into the bedroom.

I let out a sigh. I prayed this trip would help her work out whatever she was going through emotionally, since she couldn't talk about it with me. And hopefully by the time I got there, my Moxie would be back in full force.

Five

Moxie

I sat in the gynecologist's office with a bunch of other women. Most women were here for their annual checkup. There was nothing more exciting than spending a Friday afternoon with your legs in stirrups and the metal jaws of death spreading your hooha open. Good times.

But there were other women here with *the glow*. That same glow you get when you discover you're going to have a baby. I didn't have the glow. I had perpetual fear. I thought about sitting on the floor of my bathroom earlier that morning and staring at the pregnancy test, one of thirty that I purchased. I had to drink a boat full of water to make sure I had a cup full of pee to dip all the sticks in. I figured that would be easier than trying to hold and hit all the sticks while I peed.

I lined them up in rows. The ones that showed double lines on the top and the digital ones on the bottom. I had read the directions for each package. Even the Spanish instructions. Well, *positivo* and *negativo* were the only words I could read, and they were pretty damn clear when the results of the test appeared.

Why were the women on the packages always smiling and holding their stomach as if being pregnant was like winning the lottery. There needed to be a model who looked scared shitless and wailing like her dog had just died. I would volunteer to be the model because I could have sworn that I shit my pants as I looked at all the positive results.

The answer to my future was in two pink lines on a stick. Not a fortune cookie or a wish granted from a shooting star. A pee-stained stick held everything I would need to know for the rest of my life. The only things I enjoyed on sticks were fudge pops or the occasional popsicle. But those never told me if I was going to have to change shitty diapers for the next three years.

I imagined myself as a mother. The only example I had was Martha and she was as dysfunctional as they came. She had no idea how to parent. I remembered the only way she knew how to sooth me was to stick cookies in my mouth. Yes, I was already nine years old when Martha came into our lives, but eating quickly became my soothing mechanism. Therefore, the only thing I knew to do with a crying child was to stick a cookie in their mouth. For someone without teeth, this was probably non-effective.

Granted, I was forgetting an important part of the equation: Miles. I tried to remind myself that I wouldn't be alone in this. Or would I? Miles and I never discussed having kids together. Sure, I had a great relationship with Dillion, but that's because I could hide my own insecure crap from one of the sweetest souls I knew. But he was an exception. He and Miles were a package deal. Being around other kids was a different story. Ironic, since I was a teacher and around them all day. But all Miles ever heard from me about how I felt about kids was how I bitched about my students.

Miss Summers?"

"Yes?" I answered the receptionist.

"It's been a little while since we've seen you. I just need you to update your paperwork."

I walked up to the desk, and she passed me the clipboard and pen. I hesitated taking it, afraid that it was really a contract with the devil to sell my soul. Then again, I lost that battle when I binged on Snickers after I said I would never touch them again.

Turning around and going back to my seat, a beautiful looking couple had come in and sat next to the chair I had occupied just moments ago. The waiting room wasn't large, so I really didn't have an option but to sit next to them. I sat down and let out an audible sigh.

"First one?" The woman asked. She was a tiny thing, maybe five foot two with what looked to be a perfectly round basketball under her floral shirt. Even though I rubbed my stomach, it was a little presumptuous on her part to think I was pregnant. Maybe I'd just gone to Taco Bell and was trying to sooth my stomach from burrito gas pain.

"Oh, I'm not here for that. I have a… thing. You know… an itch… in a naughty spot," I said and quickly ducked my head to fill out my forms. There was no reason to lie to these people other than I was the mayor of a town called living Denial.

She leaned over to her husband and said in a low tone, "Oh, Jon, that is so cute. Look how nervous she is. Do you remember when that was us? She reminded me of how you looked when we found out we were expecting Rebecca."

Now I was just curious. They'd obviously gone through this before. I lifted my head and said, "Is this your second baby?"

Both let out a loud laugh. "Oh no. This is our seventh," she said.

My mouth went slack. This woman had pushed six watermelons out her cooch. Her vagina was probably so loose, her baby would just fall right out of her like it were shooting down a Slip'N Slide.

"Wow, seventh, huh?" These days people had two, maybe three kids, but seven? "I bet that's a lot of diapers and formula to go through."

"We use cloth diapers and I still breast feed," the woman replied.

"So number seven will be close in age to number six, huh? How far apart are they?"

45

"Our youngest child is four years old. We believe that all our children will wean when they are ready."

Still breast feeding at four years old? When you're old enough to belly up to the bar and serve yourself a cold one, that's when the bartender needed to shout out last call. I had visions of a teenager walking up to their mom and saying, "Hey, Ma, I'm thirsty. Why don't I have a little snack from Titty Town.

"Miss Summers?" I looked up to the nurse calling my name. Thank God, I was afraid this woman next to me was going to ask if I wanted a milk shake.

"That's me."

The nurse led me down a hall full of pictures of babies from different sizes and origins on one side and posters of the fetus development on the other. The poster of the woman at nine months demonstrated how the baby took up all the room in the abdomen as if it were a Holiday Inn. I glanced down to my stomach; since there was already some generous padding, I would say that my baby would be living at the Ritz Carlton rather than the Holiday Inn. The nurse waved me into one of the exam rooms.

"Please step on the scale." I slipped off my shoes, stood on the scale, and closed my eyes.

"How tall are you?"

"Five feet seven inches," I answered.

The nurse scribbled down notes, not caring to look at me. The scale was digital so a number came up right away.

"So, do you want what I really weigh? Do you want my weight before I eat in the morning or after because those are two completely different numbers. Even after having a good poop that number fluctuate." I twisted my hands together. Her cold bedside manner didn't sit well with me.

She shook her head and looked up, but the corner of her lip turned down. "Let's just go with the one you feel would best describe you."

"In that case, I'm one forty-five and five foot four." I let out a little laugh. The nurse put her closed fist on her hip, which she jutted to the side.

Huffing, I said, "Fine, I'm one ninety-five."

"I'm going to take your blood pressure. I need you to roll up your sleeve."

The nurse finally looked at me as she grabbed the blood pressure cuff off the wall. She wrapped it around my arm so tight I thought my arm was going to pop off.

"Is your blood pressure always high?"

I looked over at her in confusion. "Umm, I've never been told it was high in the past."

"Well, it could be that you're carrying a little extra weight and you're nervous. You've been biting your bottom lip like you're having it for lunch."

A little extra weight? I was going to take the cuff and strangle her with it.

She noted my stats and continued with her onslaught of questions. "Looks like you haven't had your pap smear this year yet."

"No, I had it sometime last year."

She looked up from her notes. "Early last year? Midyear? End of the year?"

Who the hell was this woman? The Pap police? "Early in the year. March, I think."

"Are you on any form of birth control?" she asked, going back to her notes. "When was the date of your last menstrual period?"

My period was usually regular, but I had to think about the last time I had it.

Getting impatient, the nurse asked, "Are you on birth control?"

"I'm on the pill."

"Which one?"

I paused again, struggling to remember the brand. I usually just went to the pharmacy, opened the packet, and start popping pills. They could have been giving me cholesterol medicine and I wouldn't have known. When I became sexually active, the doctor gave me a prescription and told me to get it filled. I didn't question it because I was still horrified that a man had his hand up my pinkolicious taco. I was under the impression that a boy was supposed to at least by you dinner first. I was sixteen and stupid.

"OraPed."

She stopped writing and peered at me over her glasses. "When did you receive your last refill?"

I looked at her, tilted my head to the side, and narrowed my eyes. Why did it matter when I refilled it? "Last month."

"Mmm," she replied. "Since you think there's a chance you're pregnant, use the bathroom down the hall and to the left, pee into this cup, and put it in the little door in the wall of the bathroom. A nurse will take it from there. Then come back to this room and put this gown on."

"Damn, if I'd have known I would get this gown, I could have worn it to the clubs last weekend." I laughed, but quickly stopped when Nurse Ratched remained stone-faced.

I took the cup and headed down the hallway to the bathroom. When I got situated and ready to pee, nothing would come out. It was as if my pee suddenly got scared and crept back up into my bladder. I turned on the faucet hoping the sound of running water would help. I even spoke softly to my bladder, telling it that if it behaves, I'll treat it to a nice Coke afterward.

Luckily, my bladder complied. I had a feeling that if I didn't get something out, Nurse Ratched would come and sit on my bladder. I put the cap on the cup and opened the little door to place my specimen. I looked at the cup before I shut the door. It was all very metaphorical. One door closes and another opens. Except this door was closing on sanity and opening the door to a fucking black hole.

A few minutes after I'd returned to the exam room and put on the gown, there was a knock at the door. I was expecting to see my regular doctor, but unless Dr. Chandler went through gender reassignment and turned into a rock star god, I was pretty sure this wasn't her. This was a living Greek sculpture with dark brown hair and even darker eyes. His jaw was so chiseled and perfect, I wanted to lick him like a lollipop. Even though he was beautiful, he also looked fresh out of medical school.

"Miss Summers?"

My mouth lacked the ability to move or close, for that matter.

"I'm Dr. Ford." He held out his hand, but my arm couldn't move either.

"Where is Dr. Chan-Chan-Chandler?" Apparently I'd picked up a stutter in the last thirty seconds.

He dropped his hand, his perfectly trimmed eyebrows knitting together. "Dr. Chandler retired. Didn't you get the letter?"

I probably did get the letter, but figured it was a bill, stuffed it somewhere, and pretended it never came or miraculously paid itself.

"Umm, no, I guess I didn't," I said, feeling a little sheepish.

"Is this okay if I do the exam?" A little worried crease marred his otherwise flawless features.

I needed to get myself together. "Of course it is. I've just never had a male doctor before."

"I can assure you, Ms. Summers, once you've seen one, you've seen them all. Nothing surprises me."

"Nothing? I'm sure you don't get many clowns in full makeup dropping their pants for you." I laughed.

With a completely straight face, he said, "When I examined her, she would beep her nose every time I tried to stick the speculum in."

That's all it took. I instantly relaxed; thankful Dr. Ford had a sick sense of humor like me.

"I would hate to hear what happened during a breast exam."

He sat on the rolling chair and grabbed my file off the table, looked it over, and then back at me. His brown eyes were soft and caring even though he looked young enough to be one of my student teachers. There was a knock at the door and Nurse Ratched came back in and handed Dr. Ford a piece of paper. If I was not mistaken, she shook her head and she left the room. What was with the stick up her ass? Maybe one of the doctors lost their speculum.

Dr. Ford read the piece of paper then looked at me, a wrinkle between his brows. "Moxie, you said that you are on the pill? Which pill are you on?"

"OraPed," I said, annoyed that I had to go over this information again.

Dr. Ford gave me the same expression that Nurse Ratched gave me.

"Who put you on that pill?"

"Doctor Chandler did. Why?" I was starting to worry a little at his tone.

"Moxie, there are two things I need to tell you. First thing is that you are indeed pregnant."

"I kinda of got that by the thirty pregnancy tests I took."

"Thirty?"

"You never know, some could have been faulty."

"Well, that's funny that you should bring up the word faulty." He closed my file. "As I'm sure you know the pill isn't hundred percent effective. But in your case it was even less so. In the past six months, there was a mandatory recall on OraPed. There was a problem with the package design at the factory which caused a screw up with the order the pills that were placed in the package. In the current pack you were probably taking the placebos when you thought you were taking the regular pills."

My mouth unhinged once again. I was going to find the factory where the pills were made and set it on fire. For all I knew it was a sweatshop run by twelve-year-old kids who thought it would be funny to get unsuspecting women pregnant.

"Moxie, are you still with me?"

"Yup. Just thinking about arson and pharmaceutical companies."

"Umm, okay, then. Why don't you lay back, and we'll take a look at you. We will be able to discuss your options."

"Does one of my options include a return policy?" I mumbled as I lay back on the table.

The Pregnancy Guide

Month 1-2

Women

Congratulations, you're pregnant! Your body is getting ready to transform into a wonderful living space for the newest member of your family. While many women don't experience any symptoms the first month, some women experience sore breasts, tiredness, and some mood swings. Things that will come in handy during this time are saline spray for that stuffy nose, saltines for nausea, and stool softeners for constipation. What is commonly known as morning sickness can be felt anytime of the day. Eat what you can and let your man pamper you. You might experience headaches and an increased sense of smell. You might also feel the amplified need to urinate and to pass gas.

Men

Do you remember that smoking hot bombshell you wanted to bang all day long? Yeah, you can kiss her good-bye. Her boobs? They're going to get huge! But... you won't be touching them. That's right; those nice voluminous masterpieces will be off limits for the next nine months. If you try to touch them, you might get your hands torn off. You know that sweet woman who you used to live with? Her name will be changed to Satan. Don't expect to go into the bathroom anytime in the near future. She will be living in there, trying to take a shit. Oh, the puke! It won't stop. It will be like a steady stream coming out of your loved one's mouth. Offering saltines and ginger ale will only result in you getting a ginger ale enema. That excuse of "not tonight, I have a headache," will be a permanent statement around the house. Remember that new cologne you got for your birthday? You can throw that out. Along with your soap, shampoo, and favorite foods. Make sure that a bathroom will be within five feet of your current location because her bladder will become running a faucet. Invest in a gas mask. Mustard gas is wimpy compared to the stuff coming out of her ass.

Six

Moxie

Renee, Ryan, Dillion, and I boarded the plane to Florida. I hated airlines for a multitude of reasons. The cramped leg room, seat mates who thought it was fun to play elbow war on the arm rest, and passengers who thought they could get away with passing gas without anyone noticing. Back in the day, flight attendants offered pillows and blankets along with iffy-looking food served on steel trays that you were scared to eat, but ate anyway because it was cool.

Now, thanks to investigative news stories, we discovered there was poop particles on the pillows and blankets with crabs. You even had to fork over your credit cards to get a two-ounce bag of peanuts, which you can't eat because a majority of the plane had a nut allergy. Therefore, getting on a plane wasn't something I looked forward to.

Luckily, we all had seats together. Except Ryan. He sat in the adjacent row because there were only three seats in the row. Unfortunately for him the man sitting next to him forgot his deodorant and sweat like a racehorse after the Kentucky Derby. The armpits of his dress shirt were soaked through and he patted the beaded perspiration from his balding head with a napkin.

"Sir, are you okay?" Ryan asked after buckling himself in.

"Yeah, don't mind me. I'm just a nervous flyer," the sweating man said.

"Well, I'm sure everything will be fine. You know there are more accidents in cars than there are on planes." Ryan shrugged and waved off the man's concerns.

"That's why I don't drive," the man replied in a shaky voice.

"It's amazing you even leave your house," Ryan mumbled, turning so he faced us as much as he could in a restrained plane seat.

Renee, Dillion, and I were stuffed into our seats. Dillion insisted on bringing his pillow from home and wanted the window seat so he could look out and watch the clouds. I ended up in the middle, feeling like sausage, while Renee had it nice and easy in the aisle and could extend her legs out, even though she was rifling through her purse, which was big enough to stash an entire grocery store in. I put up the armrest, hoping to gain one more inch in both directions.

I leaned over to Renee. "Can you please explain to me why it's three hundred dollars per ticket just so we can be herded on here like cattle?"

"Something about the airlines being strapped for money." She took out her magazine from her bag.

"At this rate we might be better off traveling by horse-drawn covered wagon."

"Maybe we should play the Oregon Trail game," she added.

"Instead of forking over money for these stupid bags of peanuts, we'll have to hunt squirrel, and we both know that squirrel would only satisfy me for thirty seconds. Also, one of us would die from dysentery."

"What's dysentery?" She scrunched her nose up and furrowed her eyebrows.

"It's when you have really bad poop and can die," Dillion chimed in.

Renee and I looked at Dillion in surprise. "Okay, first of all, I shouldn't really be surprised that he knew that. Second, it's really a problem you don't know what dysentery is considering you're a fifth grade teacher."

"I thought normal people called it the stomach flu." Renee shrugged.

"No. What you had last week when you kept running to

the bathroom to vomit was the stomach flu. I thought the principal was going to call hazmat team to clean up after you." Thinking about that day only made me feel worse.

I turned to Dillion. "I better text your dad to let him know we got on the plane and are ready for takeoff."

"Tell him we are on a Super 80 aircraft and our destination is 1,153 miles." He bounced in his seat, smiling.

It never ceased to amaze me how much knowledge Dillion could fit into his brain. Even though he was only in first grade, he could easily be accepted into Harvard next year. I'll have to talk to Miles about getting his enrollment papers ready.

"Excuse me, ma'am, can you buckle your seat belt?" The flight attendant pointed to my lap.

"Of course." I latched the belt and pulled out my phone to send Miles a quick text.

> *This is Minnie Mouse talking from the cockpit. We'll have lift-off in three minutes.*

> *Minnie, this is Mickey. Glad you got on the plane okay. How's Dillion?*

"Excuse me, ma'am, you'll have to shut off all your electronic devices now." The flight attendant's mouth was a thin line and her eyes shot imaginary laser beams at my head.

"Umm, sure. No problem."

I pretended to turn it off and put it away. As soon as she

was a few rows up, I took my phone out again and continued my text to Miles.

> *He's great. Really excited and so am I. I'm enjoying playing pretend mommy. It's fun.*
>
> *Who says you're pretending anything? You're going to be a mommy sooner…*

"Ma'am."

I looked up at the flight attendant I now referred to as stealth ninja flight attendant, or SNFA for short, as she eyed me like a disobedient child.

"You need to shut off the phone right now. I've asked you once already."

"Yeah, sorry. I just have to finish reading this really important text from my boyfriend," I said, sticking out my lower lip for sympathy.

"Ma'am, the captain really doesn't want to hold up the entire flight just so you and your boyfriend can play text footsie. I'll stay right here to make sure you put it in airplane mode properly."

Was she kidding me? Who the fuck did this woman think she was? More importantly, what did the rest of Miles's text say? Did he know something about my pregnancy? I took the pregnancy tests in my apartment so he wouldn't see them. Did he find out somehow? Was that why he sent us on this trip, to stage an exit plan to leave me? Bile rose in my throat. But then why would he send Dillion with me? Oh my God, he's going to leave me to raise Dillion and move to the Antarctic.

My hands shook as I turned off my phone for takeoff. I closed my eyes and thoughts of having to raise Dillion and a new baby all by myself crept into my mind. How would I do it? Dillion and this baby would hate me forever, and I didn't have enough money in my retirement plan to send them both to therapy?

"Moxie, are you okay? You're sweating as bad as the guy sitting next to Ryan." Renee looked at me with concern.

"Are there barf bags in here?" I dug behind the magazines in the seat pocket in front of me.

"Seriously? You haven't even been drinking?"

"It's not that. But I think I'm going to be sick."

"This is a piss-poor time to get the flu. Don't tell me I have to go on Space Mountain by myself. Ryan is too much of a pussy to go with me."

"It's not the flu." I leaned back in the seat and closed my eyes.

"I knew it. Ryan poisoned you with his sad excuse of blueberry muffins this morning. While it was a sweet gesture for him to bring some for us at the airport, they did taste a little off."

"I'm sitting in the aisle next to you, bitch," Ryan said from his seat

"Knowing you, you probably forgot to wash your hands after wiping your ass before making those muffins." She smiled brightly and then blew him a kiss. He gave her the finger.

I checked on Dillion. Thankfully he had his earbuds in and was probably listening to the audio book, *Tale of Two Cities*. He was talking about listening to all the great classics before he got into the fourth grade. My Dad had to pay me off to get me to read one classic book in high school so my teacher wouldn't fail me. I was glad Dillion had the capacity to entertain himself because I really feeling ill.

"While I think we should all question Ryan's culinary skills, it's not food poisoning either." I groaned, trying to keep the vomit at bay.

Renee whispered, "It's the guy in front of us, isn't it? He has enough cologne on to make a department store perfume counter jealous. I'm even ready to gag myself."

"It's not him, although I would have to tend to agree that whatever he is wearing is more offensive then a hooker airing out her underwear."

"Then what the hell is wrong—" Renee froze and stared at me for what seemed to be an eternity. Then her eyes went as big as saucers. "Noooo," she whispered, looking at me as if I had just farted.

"What's wrong?" Ryan looked up from his *GQ* magazine.

"Moxie has a minion!" Renee squealed and shook with excitement.

"I know. She has twenty-two of them she tries to control in her class. And does a pretty crappy job, if you ask me." Ryan winked.

"No, stupid! Moxie's knocked up!"

"What!" Ryan shouted so loud people turned to look in our direction.

"What? Is the plane going down? Are we going to die? Can I call my mother?" The sweaty man yelled.

"Is there a problem over here?" SNFA glided down the aisle.

"No—" Ryan started to say.

"Yes! This man said the plane is going down!" Sweaty man said, his voice cracking as he squeezed his eyes shut.

"I did not!" Ryan said.

"Moxie, I need to go to the bathroom." Dillion tugged on my arm, immune to the confusion.

"Okay, I'll take you."

"I'm sorry, ma'am, you cannot get out of your seats," SNFA said stiffly.

"But he has to go to the bathroom," I replied.

"Ma'am, the fasten seatbelt sign is on." She pointed to the lit up sign on the ceiling.

"The good news is that my eyesight is working," I said to the flight attendant. "The bad news is that you're about to have a puddle on the floor if the kid can't get to the bathroom." Dillion was holding his crotch and doing the famous pee dance.

"If you take him, you're going at your own risk."

"Risk of what? Slipping on a bag of peanuts?

"Moxie…" Dillion was tugging on my shirt with force.

The flight attendant put a hand on each seat in the aisle, blocking the way to the bathroom with her body. This was not the Cold War people. I would take her body down like the Berlin Wall.

"Come on, sweetie," I said to Dillion.

I unbuckled both of our seatbelts and we crossed over Renee's legs into the aisle. A woman a few rows in front of us got up at the same time and entered the bathroom.

"You have to be kidding me," I muttered. I was convinced that woman slipped the flight attendant a hundred dollar bill to buy her silence.

"Ma'am, you can't stand in the aisle, you will have to return to your seats," SNFA said.

"But that woman took our bathroom!"

"I'm sorry. You'll have to return to your seats until the lavatory is unoccupied."

"I only have five dollars, but after the plane lands I'll find an ATM and give you five hundred dollars."

The flight attendant didn't move, and I wondered if she was born with that unrelenting stare or if it developed over time.

I turned around and whispered to Dillion, "I need you to pretend to cry."

"Why?" he asked through gritted teeth.

"Because the flight attendant Nazi isn't going to let us go to the bathroom unless we stand against the empire."

"Kind of like *Star Wars*."

"Right, you're Luke Skywalker and she's Dark Vader." I pointed to dark stewardess.

"Moxie, it's *Darth Vader*, not dark."

"To me, it's dark. I mean the woman is dressed all in black, for Pete's sake."

"I don't think I can pretend cry. I'm not feeling it."

"Dillion, this is no time to work on your method acting."

"Excuse me, is there a problem here?"

A tall well-dressed man approached us, frowning and rubbing his forehead.

I eyed his crisply pressed sport coat. "A little overdressed to go to Disney, are you?" I smirked at him.

"Miss, I suggest you still down.

"Last time I checked this wasn't your business." I narrowed my eyes and folded my arms.

"All things that happen with air transportation are my business," he said in an unpleasant tone.

"Really? Do you own the plane? Last time I checked I paid way too much to fly commercial. If I were on a private jet,

I'd be getting a foot message while someone fed me grapes."

The nausea I had felt only worsened when he reached into his back pocket and pulled out a card.

"You're an air marshal." I clutched my stomach and started to rock back and forth.

The people in the front row said something about an air marshal onboard and it raced back to each row. Now I had a better understanding of how wildfires spread. The front row was the kindling and the rest of the plane was dry wood and underbrush.

"Oh my God, there is an air marshal on the flight!" screamed the sweaty man. "That means someone on the No-Fly List is on board. We're all going down!"

People started to panic as the din of worried voices grew louder.

"Everyone calm down!" said the marshal. "We take flights routinely as a safety measure. No one is in harm's way on this flight."

"I don't know about that," I managed to say before my stomach emptied on the air marshal.

Seven

Moxie

After a discussion with the TSA and American Airlines about not harassing the flight crew, we headed to our hotel on the Disney property. We figured staying on the Disney grounds would be best so we didn't have to rent a car. The downside, however, was being herded like cattle on Disney transportation buses and sharing everyone's body odor. I wasn't exactly thrilled with the idea of smelling someone who had baked in the sun all day.

Dylan was out cold soon after we settled in the room. Renee, Ryan, and I sat in the connecting room and discussed my pregnancy. I told them about the thirty pregnancy tests and that my new doctor was Doogie Howser. We also talked about my fear that Miles would leave me. Renee told me that if I wasn't with child, she'd smack me so thoroughly they would find pieces of me all over the Disney property. Ryan added to Renee's threat and told me I must have lost brain cells on the flight because Miles and I could never be separated. After a two-hour therapy session with my besties, I finally was able to relax enough to sleep.

I woke up the next morning wrapped up like a mummy in my sheets. Dillion was still fast asleep in the bed next to mine. His hair was a disaster and his mouth was slightly open while he snoozed. He looked so much like his father. I wondered if this baby would look like Miles or if it would have flaming red hair like me. Gingers were cute as babies, but I was called *fire crotch* mercifully as a preteen.

"Good morning." Renee swept in with a singsong voice like Snow White. I waited for those dumb ass birds to come swooping in through the window and land on her finger. The problem was I felt more like one of the seven dwarfs: Pregnant Grumpy.

"Cinderella, go fetch my coffee and slippers." I flicked my hand in her direction as I rolled over in bed. That movement started waves of nausea, rippling through my stomach.

"You can't drink coffee, Miss Preggo, and get your own damn slippers."

I looked over my shoulder. She sat on the edge of the bed dressed and ready for the day. We needed a discussion about the necessities of sleeping in. "I had this dream last night that I was a dungeon master and I had Miles in chains. I was whipping him with baby blankets and making him suck on a pacifier."

"I don't know if that sounds horrifying or kinky. Do you really think Miles is going to run the other way when you tell him you're pregnant?"

"I have no idea. He's caring, receptive, and has been my number two to my number one. But we don't live together, and we haven't even brought up the M word."

"Masturbation?"

"Yes, twat waffle, masturbation. How'd you guess?" I threw one of the pillows at her. "Marriage! We haven't even gotten that far. And now I'm pregnant with a cross between an angel baby and Satan's spawn."

"Moxie, I don't think you have anything to be afraid of except your vagina stretching out too much after delivery. Miles's penis will get lost and need turn by turn directions."

"Oh my God. I'm going to have a cavern for a vagina." I slapped my hands on my face.

"Just try not to poop on the kid when you give birth. I heard women shit when pushing out the baby."

With my face still buried in my hands I moaned. "Great, I'm going to have a shitty baby."

"Why don't we go out, see the parks, ride the rides, and get your mind off this for a bit."

"All right. I just have to wake up Dillion from his coma.

He was so excited about meeting the Owl from *Winnie the Pooh* that he tired himself out."

"There was an owl in *Winnie the Pooh*?"

"Apparently. I didn't have the heart to tell him he probably got swept under with the rug with other Disney characters they didn't want to admit they created," I said as I pulled my hands away from my face.

"Like that horrible movie *The Fox and the Hound*," Renee said.

"Silence!" I held my hand up to stop her from continuing. "I told you never to bring up that horrible tale of the dog and fox again. It always makes me cry. I swear I think Walt Disney sat in his office and thought about all the different ways he could send children to therapy."

Renee laughed. "Okay, I'll get Ryan up. It'll take him forty minutes just to style his hair."

I dragged myself out of bed and washed up. No point scaring poor Dillion with dragon breath when I woke him. After I was done in the bathroom, I crept over to his bed and looked down at my favorite little boy. My mind wandered to the future and Dillion trying to teach his younger sister or brother the alphabet or physics. Right as I was about to wake Dillion there was a knock at the door.

"Who is it?" I asked. But there was no answer. I looked through the peep hole and no one was standing there. I opened the door and saw a small box with a red ribbon tied around it sat on the floor. It felt heavy when I picked it up and brought in the room. I intrigued about what the contents could have been. I giggled to myself imagining someone placing a Dumbo sized shit in a box and doing a ding, dong ditch.

A small tag was hanging from the ribbon which was addressed to Ms. Summers. I pulled the ribbon and opened the lid of the small box. There was an envelope with Moxie written in familiar handwriting along with a snow globe that contained Cinderella's castle. I shook the globe and little specks of glitter surrounded the water in the glass. I took the envelope and tore it open and read what it said.

Moxie,

I'm sorry I couldn't be with you and Dillion on your magical adventure. Since I can't be there, I had the hotel set up a special breakfast for you in one of the suites for you, Dillion, Renee, and Ryan. Even though I can't be there let this snow globe remind you that you will always be queen of the castle and of my heart.

I love you,

Miles

Tears welled up in my eyes because I'd rather have Miles here then any gift or special breakfast. But just the thought of going through all this trouble warmed my heart, and fucked with my hormones. Since Miles had set up this breakfast, I needed to get Dillion up so we could eat and get to the parks.

"Dillion." I rubbed his shoulder, glad he didn't have one of his night terrors last night. The post-traumatic stress he suffered from the car accident still lingered after all this time. It tore my heart apart. He might have healed physically from the accident, but emotionally he still carried it with him every day. Miles had gotten him into some therapy and it certainly helped him deal with reliving the car accident. Dillion had talked about breaking glass, seeing his mom covered in blood, and a man rushing out of a car to see if they were all right.

"Is it time to see the Owl?" he asked.

"I think the Owl migrated north, but Mickey Mouse will be there."

"I suppose I can take the consolation prize."

"Come on, sleepy head. Let's get ready. We're going to a special breakfast where we can indulge in enough Mickey waffles, bacon, and eggs until we puke."

That's all it took for Dillion to bolt out of bed and into the bathroom. I chuckled at the dust cloud he left behind. My stomach was queasy like it was sinking, and my nerves were fried like a bad piece of Kentucky Fried Chicken.

"That's what you're wearing?" Ryan asked as he sauntered into the room. I looked down at myself. What was wrong with my Bermuda shorts and "I'm Goofy" T-shirt?

"I figured I'd save my Cinderella gown for when we went to the ball," I said as I curtsied. "I want to be comfortable. We're going to be doing a lot of walking, and I need room for my stomach to expand with all the crap we're going to eat."

"But you look so… casual." Ryan wrinkled his nose.

"Listen, not everyone owns the whole J.Crew catalog," I said. Ryan's immaculate ensemble consisted of pressed cargo shorts, a white linen shirt, and driving loafers. He topped the whole thing with a fedora. I rolled my eyes.

"A fedora? Really?"

"If Perry the Platypus can get away with wearing one, so can I. How are you feeling, Mama?" he asked as he came up and patted my stomach.

"If you want to continue to use your hands, I suggest you remove them at once." I gave him the death glare.

"Touchy, touchy. Do we have to put up with this for nine months?"

"Unless you plan on squeezing something the size of an elephant out of something the size of a lemon, I'd advise you shut up before you lose one of your nuts."

Ryan grabbed himself. "Listen, my nuts are precious. They could one day hold the special sperm that might create the perfect human specimen."

"And who are you going to get to be a surrogate for this magical child?" I cocked an eyebrow and folded my arms.

"It's called immaculate conception, Moxie, get with the program. The baby will just appear out of thin air like Jesus."

"Ryan, I'm a Jew and even I know the story didn't happen that way." I shook my head and he turned to the mirror to admire his outfit.

Renee came back into the room armed with a camcorder, a digital camera, and her phone. I wanted to ask if she was quitting her job to become an official photographer for Disney. Except, I think they call them cast members because God forbid they be called them employees like the rest of us. Dillion finished getting ready and the four of us headed to suite 531, as instructed, for breakfast. We entered the suite, which had a large dinning area and two hotel staff members there waiting for us. The table was set with a white table cloth, four place settings and beautiful flower arrangement in the center. We all took our seats and I could see Dillion anxiously awaiting his Mickey waffles because he started bouncing in his seat and stuffed the cloth napkin in his shirt like a bib.

A staff member came to my side with a steaming pot. "Would you like some coffee, miss?"

I stared at the pot like it was water and I was a dying woman in the desert. Then I looked down at my abdomen and silently cursed the growing child because mommy couldn't have her caffeine IV drip. "Do you have…" I swallowed hard before the next word came out. "Decaf?"

"Yes, let me get you some."

Even my precious coffee didn't seem all that appetizing with the nausea I was having. But at least I would try to enjoy it going down before it came back up again. The staff served everyone food which consisted of Dillion's much anticipated waffles, scrambled eggs, bacon, and fruit. I slowly nibbled on a Mickey waffle while everyone stuffed their faces like it was the Last Supper. Even though I couldn't fully enjoy the experience, I loved Miles for going to such great lengths to make us happy.

A soft knock came from the door and one of the staff went to open it. In came what I could only describe as dollar store rendition of Mickey's best dog pal, Pluto. This person was wearing yellow sweatpants, a matching sweatshirt, yellow gloves, tennis shoes, and a black felt string attach to the ass with duct tape. To make the situation worse, they were wearing a plastic Pluto head that looked like it was purchased at a Halloween store. It reminded me of those stupid unicorn heads that guys wore at frat parties because they thought they were the coolest ones there.

Dysfunctional Pluto came over to our table and waved at everyone without saying a word. I looked at Renee and Ryan, who were sitting opposite of Dillion and I at the table. Both of them were trying hard to suppress their laughter. Renee waved back at him, and I just looked at Dysfunctional Pluto like he had the plague. Dillion jumped out of his seat and ran over to hug Pluto, and I wanted to pull him back because I thought for sure this person was hiding a weapon somewhere and was about to massacre us. Maybe Miles couldn't pay the upgrade charge to bring in a real Pluto so they had to substitute with Pluto's mentally disturbed cousin, Sudo.

Sudo surrounded Dillion in a king-sized hug. He then gave Ryan a handshake and patted Renee on the head. When he came to me, he pulled me out of my chair. He took the long tongue that hung disturbingly out of his mask and made a huge slurping sound as he drew his plastic tongue up from my chin to the top of my head.

"Wow. Thanks, Pluto. That was sweet." I patted him on the shoulder, but he wasn't finished. He took his gloved paws and engulfed me in a hug and hooked one of his legs around mine.

He finally released me and signaled to Renee to take our picture. He stood behind me and once again wrapped his giant paws around my waist. His large plastic head rested on my shoulder.

"Pluto, I know you're a horny dog, but this is the last time I'm warning you to keep your paws to yourself."

Then Sudo quickly grabbed my butt and gave a tight squeeze.

"That's it!" I said through my teeth. I turned around and kneed him right in his big doggie balls.

Renee and Ryan gasped as Sudo fell to his knees, grabbed his puppy pals, and let out a moan.

"Jesus Christ, Moxie!" Sudo said, still on his knees.

"What the fuck!" I covered my mouth with both hands. "Miles?"

"Is it always your reaction to knee Disney characters in the crotch?" Miles stood, still wincing.

"You we're groping me! What are you doing here dressed up as sudo Pluto?" My hands were in my hair and my eyes went wide. "I thought you were stuck at home working?"

"It's supposed to be a surprise. It was all planned," Miles said, his voice sounding less strained.

I turned around to look at Ryan and Renee. "You knew?"

They both nodded, biting their lips to try to contain their laughter.

"What about you?" I eyed Dillion.

"I was told that if I said anything to you, Daddy would cancel my subscription to *National Geographic.*"

"I still might cancel your subscription. Hasn't anyone taught you it's not nice to lie?" I admonished, but Dillion kept smiling because he knew I was the one lying.

"This is so sweet, Miles. But you didn't have to do all of this. You could have just come with us on the plane like a normal human being."

"Then it wouldn't have been as memorable." He put his gloved dog paws on his hips.

"Why does it have to be memorable? It's just a… Oh, shit!" It hit me like a lightning bolt.

Miles dropped down to one knee and took my hand in his fake dog paw. "Moxie, from the moment I met you, you surprised me at every turn. I love how honest you are, caring, and even how outspoken you are. You make Dillion and I complete with your love, and I want you to make our family complete. I love you, sweetness. Will you marry me?"

Ryan handed Miles a black box, and Miles, having some issues using his gloved hands, opened it to reveal and large solitaire princess cut diamond. Everything I wanted and dreamed about were at my fingertips. I wanted a future with Miles and Dillion more then I wanted my next breath. Tears rolled down my cheeks, and I clutched my stomach with my hands.

"Moxie, this is the most quiet I've ever seen you. Can you please say something so I know that you're still breathing?" Miles held the ring in front of him.

I looked at the ring and then back to Miles, his eyes filled with tears. This was the moment of fight or flight. "Miles, I'm pregnant."

Eight

Miles

Time and space froze. I remembered being in a similar situation eight years ago when my deceased wife told me she was pregnant with Dillion. When Sarah told me, I was elated and fucking terrified in the same moment. This, however, was playing out differently than that memory. This time I was dressed in a smelly Pluto costume, sweating my ass off, and on my knees proposing with broken balls. A baby? Wasn't the saying "first comes love, then comes marriage, then comes baby in the baby carriage?" I wasn't the type of guy who was all about following societal rules. I just wasn't expecting this.

"Miles? Miles? Are you still breathing?"

It was Ryan talking to me, but I couldn't be bothered to respond when I was focused solely on the beautiful redhead in front of me, looking very upset. She had her arms crossed over her chest and an aggravated line creased between her brows. We were having a baby! Why would she be upset? My sweetness was carrying a part of both of us inside of her. The caveman in me wanted to go around to everyone and yell, "I marked her, she mine! Me, Tarzan!"

"Congrats, Moxie. I think you broke him." Ryan patted my back.

His comment struck me as funny, and I started laughing uncontrollably.

But the next thing happened so fast. Moxie bolted from the suite. I was left on the floor, holding the ring box in my paw. I called after her but it was no use. This was not how I'd expected this proposal to go. A month's worth of planning— calling Disney World and begging them to let me set up this proposal—all down the crapper. Everything was perfectly organized and just like my life with Moxie so far, nothing ever went as planned.

"Dad, I think you fucked up."

I whipped around to look at my son. Dillion had never sworn in his life.

"I just heard Uncle Ryan whisper it to Aunt Renee. I thought you'd want to know just in case you did fuck up and didn't realize it."

I glared up at Ryan who was looking everywhere except me. "Did you know about the baby?" I asked the trio.

"We just found out ourselves on the way here." Renee said, casting her eyes down and nibbling her bottom lip.

"I'll see if she went to the room and talk to her. Why don't you guys go ahead to the park, and we'll meet you there later," I said.

"What makes you think she's going to forgive your sorry ass for laughing at her after she told you she was pregnant?" Renee put her hands on her hips, giving me Grade A attitude.

"I didn't mean to laugh. It was a nervous reaction."

I took a room key from Renee and headed to the elevators. When the doors opened, a young couple stood in matching Mickey and Minnie wedding hats. *Oh, the irony.* I imagined that would be Moxie and I one day, although, she would probably argue against the Minnie hat and get Winnie the Pooh just so she could say she had Pooh on her head. I chuckled, thinking how desperately I loved this woman, the woman carrying my baby.

The young couple looked me up and down, confused at my appearance. "I was trying to surprise my girlfriend. Wasn't it an impressive idea?" I asked.

"Yeah, dude," the new groom said. "But it's kind of like finding out that Santa isn't real. Ignorance is bliss, man."

I rolled my eyes just as the elevator came to my floor. I walked off, looked at the room numbers, dragged my big floppy feet to the room, and knocked on the door.

"Moxie?" I heard shuffling inside. "Baby, let me in. We need to talk."

"Why? So you can laugh at me more? Last time I checked, you were the asshole dressed up like a dog. Maybe you should go to your dog house and lick your own bone, because you sure as hell are not getting it licked by me."

"Moxie, I wasn't laughing at you. I was laughing because nothing in our relationship ever goes as planned. With you, every turn is a mystery, and that isn't a bad thing. Granted, I thought our lives together would take a more traditional route, but I shouldn't be surprised that this was meant for us."

The lock twisted and the door opened slightly. Moxie stuck her head out, her red hair all over the place and her blue eyes rimmed with tears.

"Please, sweetness. Let me in," I said quietly, resting my paw on the doorframe.

She opened the door to let me in and I studied her features. How was it possible that a person could transform within a short time. Before Moxie was my girlfriend. This crazy, lovable, outspoken spitfire was now a vulnerable woman. Was she worried that she was going to do this alone? Was she scared there would be something wrong with the baby? I wanted her to understand that as long as I was breathing, she would never be alone.

She turned her back to me and walked to the window facing Magic Kingdom. She wrapped her arms around her stomach as if to protect our baby. From what? Me?

"Turn around."

"I can't," she said, her voice shaking

I leaned in close enough to whisper in her ear. "I don't know what you're thinking, but whatever it is, you need to stop."

She finally turned and looked at me, pain etched in her eyes. "In case you didn't hear me downstairs let me repeat it for you: I'm pregnant. I'm sorry that I don't have a sign language translator with me for you to understand because apparently you didn't hear me through your laughter."

"You're right. Maybe we both need interpreters because I asked you to marry me and you ran off."

She stood there, mouth hanging open and eyes ready to pop out of her head. She stepped closer to me and poked my chest.

"I told you I'm pregnant, and you have the nerve to scold me for leaving your proposal?" she hissed.

I fired back. "You left me kneeling in a dog costume, holding a ring. A ring I had designed just for you, by the way, while you went to go have your little temper tantrum."

"I was not having a temper tantrum!" Her voice grew louder. "I was pissed because you were laughing at me."

"I was pissed I had to stand there with my balls overheating in this costume! At any rate, this might be our only kid because my nuts are oven roasted!"

We'd never fought like this before, and we both struggled to catch our breath. I took my paw and placed it on her cheek. She looked up at me, her eyes mixed with different emotions. I knew she was scared. She didn't have to tell me. Moxie used anger to push people away. It's the only way she'd learned to protect herself. She could get mad and scream at me all she wanted, but I was never letting her go.

"Moxie, I love you. I want to fucking marry you. Yes, this baby is a surprise, but I knew that we would have kids one day. It's just a little sooner than expected."

"We never discussed it," she said.

It never even occurred to me to discuss the option of having kids with Moxie. Maybe that was naïve of me. But I saw how great she was with Dillion and how much she loved him. From the moment Dillion entered her class as a kindergartener, they had shared a special connection. She told me that even at a young age, Dillion had made his mark in the world. I could only guess Moxie's fear came from her relationship with her stepmother. Martha was not exactly the best mothering role model, having criticized Moxie for almost every move that she made. But that wasn't the Moxie I saw and that certainly had not been the way she had treated Dillion. She showed only love and support for everything he had done.

"You're forgetting something here," I said. "You are not alone and will not be doing this by yourself. You have me, Dillion, Renee, Ryan…"

"I won't?" She sniffled.

Was the baby sucking the intelligence out of her head?

Where did she think I was going?

"Moxie, what in the hell makes you think that I wouldn't want this? I'm not going anywhere. You'll have to drag my dead body away because I'm going to hook it around your leg."

"That's disappointing."

"Excuse me?" I lifted my eyebrows and widened my eyes.

"I would have thought you'd hook your dead body around my boobs since you love them so much."

Her frown slowly twisted into a smile and relief washed over me. "You're right. When I die, I'm taking your boobs with me."

"You might not want them after this kid has had its way with them. I think for a push present, a boob job might be in order."

I laughed and took her in my arms. "We're having a baby," I whispered into her hair.

"I think it's going to be more of a demon spawn, but I'll cross my fingers and hope it has human features."

With her body pressed against me, I couldn't help but feel that familiar stir in my groin whenever she was close.

"Miles?"

"Mmm-hmm?

"Your doggy boner is growing."

"I'm looking for a place to bury it."

Her body jiggled with laughter. This only made me harder and want her more. She pulled away and I used the opportunity to seal my mouth on hers.

"So does this costume mean we are going to do it doggy style?" She humped me.

"Help me get out of this get up, and I'll take you in whatever way you want. But doggie style sounds like a good start. Followed by you sitting on the desk while I spread those sweet legs apart. And if you're a good girl, maybe I'll let you suck on my bone."

Moxie loved my dirty talk; I could see her hard nipples under her shirt. She moved behind me dropped my sweatpants and pulled my sweatshirt above my head. I felt the cool air hit my body. All I had on were my boxer briefs, and my erection strained painfully against the fabric. Moxie, stilled behind me, ran her hands down my abdomen to cup my cock. I sucked in a breath, the feeling of her hands around me was exquisite. It had only been two days since we'd been together and the sensations I felt hit me like a freight train.

"I want this," she said, as she squeezed my cock with her hand.

"So fucking take it." I turned and slammed my mouth onto hers. I flicked my tongue against her lips, demanding she open for me. I clutched her back and slid my hands to her breasts, wanting to knead them.

"Ow!" she yelled, jumping back and grabbing her breasts.

"What? Are you okay? I barely touched you."

"It's the pregnancy. My tits are sensitive."

"So I can't touch them?" I stuck out my bottom lip. Yes, I was actually pouting.

"Not unless you want me to nail you in the nuts again. My advice is for you to look at them adoringly until further notice."

"I guess I'll just have to pay extra attention to other parts of your body," I said, giving her a cocky wink and a confident smile.

"My big toe appreciates your extra attention."

"I was thinking more like the part between your legs." I nibbled a pathway from her neck down.

I opened her jeans and dragged them down to the floor. I could see how turned on she was, and it made me salivate. I lost my composure, wanting nothing more than to be buried in this woman. I grabbed the sides of her panties and with one hard tug ripped them off her body. She gasped. I guided her back on the bed and hooked one of her legs over my shoulder, opening her wide.

"All I can think about is how I want to fuck this beautiful pussy with my tongue," I said, warming her with my breath.

"So why the fuck are you still talking?" she said, breathless.

I smiled, knowing my little spitfire was back. I tasted her, grazing her clit with my tongue. Her hips jolted straight up off the bed and she cried out. I loved that I was able to do this to her body. It was the most indulgent high.

"God, Miles. More," she said as she grabbed the comforter.

I was happy to oblige and I sucked her sensitive spot into my mouth, hard. Moxie thrashed and I had to pin her legs down with my hands. I sucked, licked, and savored the wetness filling my mouth. I released her thighs and moved my hands up her body and under her shirt. I tweaked her nipples through her lace bra and she moaned even louder.

"Miles, I going to come."

The sight of her coming was like watching the best Fourth of July fireworks. I glided up her body, kissing her skin as I went. "I want to be inside of you when you come. I want to feel you squeezing me"

I pressed the head of my cock against her opening and it didn't take but a single nudge for me to slip inside because she was already so wet. Moxie started rocking her hips against me, searching for the friction she needed to get off. I moved faster.

"I'm not going to last long, I need you too fucking badly. I want you to come. I need you to come," I said, my voice strangled.

Her body started to contract and her legs squeezed around my hips. "Miles! I'm coming!"

The rush of my orgasm glided from my lower spine on up. My balls tightened almost painfully until I came, filling

First Comes Love

Moxie and giving me relief. I could have sworn I saw stars. Sex with Moxie had always been amazing, but this time it felt like something… more. I wasn't sure if it was because I found out she was pregnant, but the need to stay connected was intense.

"Yes," she said, panting hard.

"Yes, it was pretty incredible." I rested my head on her chest.

"No, you idiot. Yes, I'll marry you."

"It's because I fucked the answer out of you, isn't it?" I lifted my head and placed delicate kisses on her chin and cheek. "Nah. That was just an extra bonus." She smiled.

I took Moxie's mouth with mine and kissed the woman who was going to become my wife and the mother of my child.

"Miles, if you don't get off my sensitive tits in two seconds, I'll never let you to touch my boobs for the rest of our lives."

"That's okay," I said, rolling next to her. "Because I'm taking them with me into the afterlife."

Nine

Miles

After the chaos of the proposal, we spent the rest of the week enjoying the wonderful world of Disney. Renee, Ryan, and I took turns going on rides with Dillion while Moxie watched because the thought of moving objects made her turn the color of Jiminy Cricket. Plus, I wanted someone with her at all times to point out the closest bathroom or trashcan.

I was still in awe that Moxie was pregnant. She told me about the pill recall, and when I teased that we should sue the company, she broke into a raging crying fit. She said I was an asshole and could shove the pill pack up my ass. Apparently, Moxie wasn't at the point of thinking this concept was funny and the mood swings were not in my favor. It took an hour of massaging her feet and promising to change shit-filled diapers for a year for her to forgive me.

Renee and Ryan gave us some alone time with Dillion so we could talk about the baby and the wedding. In true Dillion form, he wanted to know exactly how a zygote became a fetus and if Moxie was going to lose the battle of city versus suburbs. Moxie spent an hour trying to convince us that raising the baby in the city would be really cool and hip. I told her I wanted my children to know what grass and trees were. She finally, although not without resistance, agreed to terminate her lease and live with us. However, she said she had no qualms about shooting anyone who uttered the word minivan. The rest of vacation went smoothly, although I thought Dillion was going to picket the Magic Kingdom until he saw Owl from Winnie of Pooh. When someone working there said the owl had to fly away, I was a little worried that Moxie was going to take one of the balloons and cause serious vocal cord damage to the man. That's when I knew it was time to get out of there.

The following Friday I came home from work and I found Moxie's car in already at the house. I went inside, expecting her to be spread out on the couch and decompressing from the workday. But Dillion was in her place, playing on his tablet.

"Hey, bud. How was school?" I put my workbag down.

Without looking up, he gave me a thumbs-up.

"What did you learn today?" I attempted to engage him in human-to-human conversation, once he got entranced with his National Geographic shows, it was like talking to a brick wall.

Dillion shrugged.

I tried again. "Did you know that they elected the first cow to be president of the United States, and I'm moving to Ecuador?"

Again, I only received thumbs-up.

I gave up on Dillion and called out for Moxie as I walked through the house. A muffled groan came from the hall bathroom.

"Moxie? You okay in there?

"Ugh, leave me alone. My destiny is to perish in the pits of hell." She moaned again.

"Sweetness, can I get you something? Some saltines or ginger ale?"

"I swear to God, if one more person offers me ginger ale or saltines, I'll give them a ginger ale enema. This is entirely your fault, you know. It's because of you and your power penis that I'm sitting here revisiting my lunch. It wasn't even that good going down; ten times worse coming back up."

Talking through a wooden door wasn't helping; I cracked the door open to see Moxie lying on her side on the tiled bathroom floor.

"What are you doing?"

She looked up from the floor. "I'm surveying the grout to see if it needs to be redone. What the fuck does it look like I'm doing? I'm dying a sad, slow death."

"What are you holding?"

She rolled herself over and I saw the familiar blue, white, and black package gripped in her hands. "Are those Oreo cookies?"

"Yes," she said, patting the bag and speaking sweetly to the cover.

"Why are you holding Oreos?" I tried very hard not to laugh because I valued my life.

"Because I miss them and it's comforting to look at them. But the smell is making me sick."

I bent down to remove the Oreos from her hands. But she clutched the bag tighter and gave me a murderous look.

"Take the Oreos and I will rip off your hands. You'll have to masturbate with your feet."

"Why would I need that when I have your mouth?" I wiggled my eyebrows. Man, I just couldn't help myself. If I kept this up, I'd need to update my will.

"Do you have a death wish?" she asked with a scoff.

Definitely updating that will.

I sat down beside her, pulled her onto my lap, and tenderly massaged her head. She let out a long sigh and the Oreo package fell from her grasp. I'd take the sickness away from her if I could. I wondered for a brief minute what it would be like if men could get pregnant. Would we be able to handle the morning sickness? The changes to our bodies...

Pushing a watermelon out our penises. I shuddered at the thought, knowing there wasn't a man on this fucking planet who could handle what women went through.

"I'm going to be a shitty mom."

"Where did that idea come from? You're amazing with Dillion."

"The other week, you were out of lunch meat so I gave him two pieces of bread with a marshmallow between them."

"We have marshmallows?"

"Umm, they must have appeared out of thin air." She shrugged, feigning innocence.

"I'm sure the other kids were jealous and wanted their moms to pack them a marshmallow sandwich. See, you'll be the cool mom."

"Yeah, right. I'll be the mom who leaves her kids stranded in the stroller because I saw a hot dog stand on the street corner and got distracted."

"I don't blame you. A good hot dog is hard to come by. Unless it's my hot dog and that's free."

She slapped my knee. "I'm serious, you ass."

I pulled her closer and kissed her hair. "I know you're serious, but I think the idea of you being a bad mom is absurd."

"You're just saying that to get into my pants."

"That's partly true. I do enjoy some quality time in your pants. However, I think if I made a move on you now, I would get puked on. And as much as I would love to reenact our first meeting, I'll have to take a pass."

An idea suddenly came to me, but I wasn't sure how Moxie would react to it. I didn't want her to feel she was inadequate when she became a mother. She suffered from a lot of self-esteem issues. I told her every day how much I loved her and I would continue to tell her. I couldn't wait to see her belly grow and hold my hand over it when the baby kicked and moved. It pained me to see her upset. I had a great upbringing with parents who loved each other and a sister I had gotten along with. Moxie grew up with Martha and that was enough to send anyone over the edge. However, this was going to change. I was taking care of her now and I knew, even if she didn't, how strong a woman she was. Sometimes you can't always accept it from those who are too close to you. I needed to approach this subject delicately.

"When Sarah died in the accident, I thought I died right along with her. Then I had to watch Dillion fight for his own life. I was a shell of the person I used to be, but I had to be strong for Dillion. There was a huge part of me that was scared I wouldn't be able to give Dillion enough, that he needed both parents to be whole. I was blessed that Dillion pulled through, but I still carried my grief and pain around. I felt that I was shortchanging him."

"But you're an amazing father," she said softly.

"I didn't feel that way, not even close. Then my mom convinced me to go see a therapist to try to work out some of my grief. She said I was useless to Dillion if I couldn't come to terms with what happened. I might not suffer with night terrors like Dillion, but I was having nightmares. I kept visualizing what Sarah was feeling and seeing when the car was hit. I had guilt that I wasn't in the car; that I couldn't be there with her and Dillion."

Moxie hung on to my every word. I was lucky that she never got jealous when I talked about Sarah. She knew Sarah had been an important part of our life. But she also knew I loved her fiercely. I was a lucky man to find love twice. But Moxie never compared herself to Sarah. She knew she didn't have to.

"What are your thoughts about seeing a therapist to work out some of these issues?" I held my breath, worried I'd overstepped.

"I think the therapist would probably be dead by the time we even began to hit the issues I need to deal with. There is a lot of ground to cover, starting with when I was two years old and decided to draw on the walls."

"I think a lot of kids that age try to draw on the walls. I wouldn't call that therapy worthy."

"But my choice of medium was the remnants of my poop-filled diaper. I think my mom decided to start potty training that day."

I couldn't help but chuckle. Moxie always knew how to make a statement, even as a toddler.

"I'll call Dillion's therapist and see if she can see you. She sees both children and adults for therapy. I'll even go with you for your first appointment if you want."

"Can I bring the Oreos?" She held the package close to her chest.

"If the smell doesn't make you vomit all over my car, you can bring anything you want," I said, smoothing her hair with my hand.

Tears streamed down Moxie's face. I panicked, thinking I'd offended her by suggesting therapy. "Sweetness, I wasn't suggesting that you're going to be a bad mom—"

"No, it's not that." She sniffled and wiped away the tears on her cheek. "I'm scared that I will never eat Oreos again!"

I smiled and patted Moxie's red locks. "Glad to see you have your priorities in check."

Ten

Moxie

Last time I attempted therapy was after my mom died, and let's just say it didn't go over to well. Dr. Whatever The Fuck—I'll call him WTF—had me come into his office that reeked of rotten cantaloupe and dead fish. He was a large man with graying hair and a silver mustache, which I swore had particles of food matted in his whiskers. He wore what I liked to refer to as *Bill Cosby sweaters*, which were knitted with a variety of colors splashed on them. This was paired with brown corduroys that also had some sort of food remnant on them. It was Martha's idea that I went to therapy. She and my father were about to get married, and she felt I had to deal with my mother's death before the wedding. My time with Dr. WTF didn't help.

WTF: "Moxie, I'm very glad you're here today. It was very brave of you to take this first step in your recovery."

Preteen Moxie: "Whatever."

WTF: "I'm so sorry to hear about your mother. It sounds like she was a fantastic woman."

Preteen "annoyed" Moxie: "Whatever."

WTF: "I understand your father is getting remarried. How does that make you feel?"

Preteen "I think I want to fuck with this guy's head" Moxie: "Oh, you mean Martha? She's cool! Did you know that she comes from the planet Zoltar? She's in charge of the little Zoltarians. I'm going to have brothers and sisters. But they won't look like me because their skin is a chartreuse color. And their noses are on top of the eyes."

WTF: "Umm, well, Moxie, that's an interesting fantasy that you have, but I think we need to talk about the reality of your father remarrying a person who is not your biological mother. That must make you have some uncomfortable feelings since you were so close to your mother."

Preteen Moxie: "You know, I do have an uncomfortable feeling."

WTF: "Tell me about them. Maybe we can explore how to overcome them."

Preteen "bored" Moxie: "I get this feeling. It's squishy

and warm and I can't sit still."

WTF: "This is good. Is it anger? Are you angry with your father for remarrying?"

Preteen "Let's hit him where it hurts" Moxie: "No, it's usually because I shit in my pants and just need a change of underwear."

Martha and my dad where called into the room and Martha was horrified I would act like such a child when she was doing everything to help me move past my grief. I reminded her I was a preteen and liked sitting in the puddle of my own grief so leave me alone.

Miles and I walked into the office of Dr. Nikki Gerber. The waiting room was calming with blue walls and soft music playing. Thankfully we were the only ones in the room. It would have made it even more uncomfortable if someone else was mentally judging me for my lunacy. However, if another person was sitting in here, I would be judging them, too. Miles reached for my hand in a gesture to sooth me, but it didn't work. I kept thinking about how the therapist would confirm I had shitty mommy instincts and the fact that bringing a child into this world was about as bright an idea as teaching apes to learn to use armed weapons. *Planet of the Apes* anyone?

An older woman with silver hair came into the waiting room, holding tissues to her eyes. She was crying.

I leaned over and whispered in his ear. "Miles?"

"Yup?"

"The therapist just made the woman from *Driving Miss Daisy* cry."

"Maybe she just had a powerful session?"

"Maybe she has pictures of dead little puppies and demands you stare at them until you confess to shit you've never done."

"I've been in there with Dillion. No dead puppies, I swear. Now the same can't be said about cats."

"That's okay. Cats are Satan's way of reminding us that there is indeed hell on earth."

Even though he didn't reply, I felt Miles shoulders shake with laughter. A smart-looking woman with black-rimmed glasses followed the elderly woman out the door. She looked classy, dressed in a black pencil skirt and crisp white blouse. She was put together, but not in an overwhelming way.

She spoke to the other woman. "Mrs. Hearth, I'm honored you shared your fears with me today. Thank you for trusting me. I look forward to seeing you next week."

Then, something beyond my preconceived notions of therapy happened: The older woman turned to the doctor and hugged her.

"Thank you, Nikki."

She stuck her tissue back into her handbag and exited the waiting room. Dr. Gerber watched her leave and then turned her attention to us.

"Hi, you must be Moxie." Dr. Gerber walked over to shake my hand. Her hand was soft and welcoming. "I'm glad that Miles called me. Why don't we start with both of you coming into the room and we can talk a little. Then I'll get to spend some one-on-one time with just you."

"Sounds good." Miles helped me stand and led me into the next room.

"What happens if I get sick?" I asked, trying to use the morning sickness card to get out of this.

"How is that different than any other day of our lives?" The corner of Miles's lips twitched upward and he gave me a wink.

"Miles's pants will make good target practice," Dr. Gerber said, smiling at me.

My eyes brightened and my lips turned upward into a smile. Was that sarcasm? Yes, I do believe it was. Dr. Gerber just might get my seal of approval after all. Those who belittled others were people I couldn't stand. But sarcasm and I were on a first name basis.

"I have three kids and was deathly sick with all of them. Men wouldn't know what to do with themselves if they had to go through what we did with pregnancy. I think God gave the wrong gender the set of balls." Dr. Gerber continued to smile as she sat in her chair.

I swore the heavens opened a shone down a beam of light on this woman.

"I don't disagree with you, Nikki. I wouldn't survive one

day of pregnancy," Miles said, shaking his head.

Since Dr. Gerber was Dillion's therapist, it was nice that she already had an established relationship with Miles. And oddly, I didn't feel threatened by that. She had done so much to help Dillion with his PTSD and had given Miles tremendous advice on how to help Dillion through his night terrors after the accident. I, on the other hand, would need a miracle to get me to a place where I felt comfortable with the idea of becoming a mom.

"Please have a seat, you two. Can I get you something to drink? Some water?"

"I'll take a Stoli on the rocks, thanks." I laughed.

Dr. Gerber laughed, too. "Trust me, Moxie, it won't be that bad. I just get into you head and tell you it's all because Freud said we're in love with our mommies."

"Well, Freud was wrong on all accounts in that case," I replied.

Miles and I sat on the couch across from Dr. Gerber, and he put his arm around my shoulders. It was his way of letting me know he was there for me, comforting me. And I loved him for it.

"So, I do believe congratulations are in order? A baby and a wedding?"

"Yup, we're doing things a little backward," I said, glancing at a floor and fidgeting with my hair.

"I think Moxie is experiencing some angst when it comes

to becoming a mom. As much as I try to reassure her, it doesn't seem to matter. She's amazing with Dillion and she's a teacher. I wish she could see the strong woman I see." He looked at me with a warm face and tucked my hair behind my ear. I think I melted in a puddle of goo. Clean up on aisle four!

"Moxie, Dillion does speak very highly of you. But I can understand your fear, and it's certainly normal to have fears about becoming a parent."

"It's not just becoming a parent," I said. "I don't exactly have the best role model."

"You don't have a good relationship with your mom?" Dr. Gerber asked.

"My mom died from breast cancer when I was nine. My dad remarried when I was ten. I only have a handful of memories of Mom, most of them being wonderful. I just think the time spent with Martha has ruined me for all my future children."

"Martha is your stepmother?"

"Stepmonster, yes."

Dr. Gerber chuckled. "I see. Miles, I would like some time with Moxie alone, and then we can meet together at the end. Is that okay?"

Miles looked at me with hesitant eyes. I nodded to him once, and he kissed my head and left the room. I clasp my hands together and started to rock slightly.

"Moxie, I want you to feel free to tell me whatever you're

comfortable discussing. I am not here to fix things. I'm just here to help you understand how your past can affect your current state and your future. However, I will not bullshit you and let you off the hook when things get tricky. If you want to move past your fears, you're going to have to put in the work."

I sat there with my mouth hanging slightly open. "Do you say bullshit to clients who are children, too?"

"No. I put it in more child friendly terms like doggy poo-poo."

Again, she gave me a warm smile, and I relaxed for the first time since walking into the office.

"Why do you think Martha has an impact on what kind of mother you're going to be?"

"Geez, doc, you don't kid around. Aren't you supposed to ask me to rate my feelings on a scale of one to ten. One being in the middle of a graveyard and ten being naked on top of millions of dollars?"

"Doggie poo-poo, Moxie."

"Fair enough," I said. "Martha and I have a very interesting relationship."

"I've figured."

"About six months after my mom died, my aunt convinced my dad to go to a singles mixer at our temple. She said it would be good for him. Those singles mixers are basically set up for gold diggers and soul suckers like Martha to swoop in on unsuspecting men and grab them with their talons. Ten months later they were married in the Rabbi's office. Martha wasn't previously married and had no children so she took me on as her pet project."

"And you didn't feel you needed another mother?"

"No, I just didn't feel like I *needed* Martha. From the second Martha and I met, it was *Clash of the Titans*. I wasn't the perfect daughter and she tried her hardest to make me fit the mold."

"How so?"

I couldn't help but snicker at the memories resurfacing. There were so many of them to pick from, but we only had an hour. "For my twelve birthday she picked me up from school and told me she was taking me for a surprise. I was actually excited, thinking maybe she'd take me to get my hair done or a mani-pedi."

"And?"

"She took me to Jenny Craig and said for my birthday it was time to transform me into the pretty swan she knew I could be."

Dr. Gerber kept quiet, letting me continue.

"When I was fourteen, she gave a boy a five dollar bill to kiss me during the snowball dance at Jeremy Swartz's Bar Mitzvah." I swallowed. "When I was sixteen and got my braces off, she asked the orthodontist what it would cost to wire my mouth shut to help me lose weight."

"So Martha has a bit of an issue with control?"

"Dr. Gerber, how much did you pay for your education?"

"Too much."

"Not enough because I could have told you Martha has control issues when I walked into the room and saved us some time."

She laughed. "Education is overrated."

"Hey, don't say that to loud, I'll lose my job." I joined her in laughter.

"Moxie, I want to do an exercise with you."

Dr. Gerber got up and walked over to her desk to get a pad of paper and a pen. She handed me the pad before sitting back down. "I want you to write a letter to the baby."

I looked at her in confusion. "A letter to the baby? And how am I supposed to deliver it? Send it up the coochie canal?"

Dr. Gerber barked out a laugh. "Not exactly. In this letter I want to tell the baby about your fears of becoming a mother."

"That's not a letter, that's a whole novel. Maybe a series of novels called, *What the Fuck Was I Thinking?*"

"Let's just start with the prologue then." She winked. "I'm going to give you some time alone while I go chat with Miles."

Dr. Gerber stepped out of the room and I stared at the pad of paper and pen. I suddenly felt like I was about to take an algebra test and forgot to study. Who was I kidding, I would never study for a math test. I hated math. I'd take the F and move on with my life. I decided that the best thing to do is just start writing.

Dear, Thing in My Uterus

Dear, Peanut-Sized Human Without Fingers or Toes

Dear, Devil Spawn Making Me Vomit Every Twenty Minutes

Hey Dude, What's up?

Yo! This is your mama

Twenty minutes passed and both Miles and Dr. Gerber came back into the room. Miles reclaimed his position next to me and kissed my shoulder as he sat down.

"So, how did it go?" Dr. Gerber asked

"Umm, well, I got the greeting down." I showed the paper to Dr. Gerber in which all I had written was hey.

Dr. Gerber smiled. "Looks like we have a lot of work in front of us."

The Pregnancy Guide

Month 3-4

Women

Good news! You've made it to the end of your first trimester. As you move through the third and fourth month of pregnancy, your fatigue and morning sickness will fade. You will notice that your midsection is growing to the size of a grapefruit and you might start to feel a fluttering or bubbling feeling which is the first indication of the baby's movement. Food cravings might start to appear, but be careful because heartburn could cause some discomfort. Your hormones start to stabilize which means you will tend to have less mood swings. Some women start to feel their sex drive returning, but don't be too hard on yourself if the desire to have sex is still unappealing.

Men

Do you feel lately that your penis is going to shrivel up and die? Or do you have blisters on your palms from masturbating to much. Yes, we understand that you barely remember what your partner's vagina looks like, but have no fear! This is the time where you just might get lucky. Try providing her with the items she craves, even if it's pickles dipped in horseradish. Hey, it's not your digestive system being destroyed. Step up and be the domestic powerhouse and offer to clean up the house. But watch out for the drool. Man, I woke up the other morning in a swimming pool and that's after not sleeping all night because of her snoring. Did you know that a woman can grow a third nipple during this time? A THIRD NIPPLE! And I'm not talking about the cool kind that you can suck and play with. Wait, weren't we talking about finally seeing her vagina again?

Eleven

Miles

I stood in front of the house where Moxie grew up. Well, at least from when she was ten years old. Martha insisted they find a new home after she married Moxie's dad. She said they needed a house where they could start over as a new family. Moxie later told me Martha swore she heard the ghost of Moxie's mom in her old house telling her what a bitch she was for marrying her husband and raising her daughter. Moxie then confessed it was really her voice Martha heard. She had made a recording of her voice on her boombox and hid the stereo in places where Martha wouldn't find it.

The house was in the northwest suburbs of Chicago. It looked like your average house, on an average street. The outside was pretty unassuming with white siding, black shutters, and a pathway that led up to the front door. Moxie once told me that Martha complained about the house they ended up in, saying that it could have been more like the house where Janice Lowenfield lived. Janice's husband was also fucking loaded.

Moxie said the neighborhood was ninety percent Jewish, and when someone who wasn't Jewish moved in, the people in the neighborhood adopted them, deeming them Jews through osmosis. They were then expected to attend all major Jewish holiday meals.

Moxie looked a little peaked. "Are you okay? Are you feeling sick to your stomach?"

"No. I feel *Martha sickness* and dread because I know what's waiting for us inside of there."

"What's that?"

"Sad and decrepit beef," she said solemnly as if she were announcing someone's death.

"Now, now. We don't need to start calling Martha names." I chuckled, hoping to lighten Moxie's mood. I know this was the last thing she wanted to do, especially since I wasn't Martha's first choice of a husband. But Moxie did love her dad, and she wanted him to know he was going to be a grandpa. I asked Moxie what the baby was going to call Martha. Her answer was simple. Devil Woman.

Moxie's expression became distant, almost as if she were in a daze. "Within those walls is the poorest excuse of Jewish delicacy. Many challah's met their death in there, along with matzo ball soup. Children's cries can still be heard in the distance because of the failed blintz and kugel."

"Is it worse then gefilte fish?"

Moxie refocused and met my eyes with her curious ones. "How do you know about gefilte fish? You're from Maine."

"There are Jews in Maine."

"That's like finding a four leaf clover in a sea of dandelions," she said as she squeezed her lips together to hide a laugh.

"So, what's so horrifying in there?" I pointed to the house, knowing that leaving Dillion with my sister was the best choice.

"Whenever there is a special occasion Martha makes brisket," she said.

"Fantastic, I love brisket. I fail to see the issue."

"I usually do too. But Martha's brisket is like having ox testicles sitting in elephant dung gravy." She stuck her tongue out, pretending to gag.

"Well, doesn't that sound appetizing."

"We'll have to make a mandatory McDonalds run after we leave."

Just as I was about to argue the fact that McDonalds probably also used ox testicles, the front door swung open. A petite woman with short brown hair styled like a football helmet stood waiting to tackle. Martha.

"There they are!" She squealed, her hands clutched together and shaking. She bounced in place, looking like a three-year-old needing the bathroom.

"Hey, Martha," Moxie said dryly.

"My daughter and her handsome beau have come home." She reached for a hug.

Moxie squeezed my hand so tight I thought she'd cut off circulation. She loathed it when Martha referred to her as her daughter. I shook my hand loose, opting to wrap my arm around Moxie's shoulders to avoid losing it to nerve damage. Martha embraced us both. I gave a small hug in return, while Moxie kept her arms to her side.

"Come in, come in. Let me see you. Your father is so thrilled you're here." She waved us into the house and closed the door behind us.

Walking into the house, I was blasted with 1980s nostalgia. There was Formica everywhere and the walls were painted a light peach. A piece of art that contained different color paint splashes lined the walls and the carpets were a cream plush. I felt as if I'd find my old stonewashed jeans and Member's Only jacket.

"So this is the boy that stole our Moxie's heart." Martha took my arms and spread them out, inspecting me for defects.

I wanted to remind her that she was the one who tried her hardest to make sure Moxie ended up with someone else, but I put the thought away and placed my arm around Moxie's shoulders.

After letting me go she went after Moxie. She stood with her arms firmly planted to her sides while Martha caged her in like an animal.

"One of the great things about hugging Moxie is that there's always lots of her to hug," Martha said in a sickening sweet voice. She let go of Moxie and tapped her nose before turning and walking into the kitchen.

Moxie pulled a Norman Bates and slashed her invisible knife in the air behind Martha. I shook my head, not at Moxie but at Martha's backhanded comment. I took Moxie's hand again, even though I feared loss of blood circulation, it was important she knew I was there to support her. This was the last place she wanted to be.

"Steve, Moxie and her boyfriend are here," Martha called from the kitchen. It irked me that she wouldn't call me by name. I was just known as the "boyfriend" as if I were temporary. She was in for one hell of a shock. My dislike of Martha stemmed from two issues, both Moxie related. First and foremost I didn't like the woman by proxy. She has been horrible to Moxie over the years. The stories I'd heard from Moxie about things Martha did to her made me cringe. Anyone, who tried to hurt the woman I desperately loved was an automatic negative on my list. But a few months ago was when my distaste really grew.

Martha had planned out Moxie's life down to who she thought she should date. She had set her up with a guy named David because he was educated, Jewish, and rich. At that time I was confused over Dillion's mental health but willing to open my heart to Moxie. I couldn't stay away if I tried. In the end, David had an ulterior motive. He wanted to use Moxie as his weight loss guinea pig. Since Martha had such an issue with Moxie's weight, if she ended up with David, then in Martha's mind, it would have killed two birds with one stone.

Clunking sounds came from the stairs as Moxie's dad came down the stairs. Moxie had his blue eyes and some of the similar facial features.

"Hi, baby girl." He gathered her into a hug and kissed the top of her head.

"Hey, Dad. What happened to the happy fat that surrounded the middle?" She patted his belly, and he let out an oomph.

"Martha's got me on a diet. Seems my cholesterol is a little high," Steve said, rubbing his belly.

I stuck my hand out. "Hello, Mr. Summers. I'm Miles Dane."

Steve adjusted his glasses and took my hand in a firm handshake. "Miles, it's a pleasure meeting you. Thank you for bringing my little girl home for a visit. It's been a while." There was a look in his eyes that I couldn't place, maybe sadness or regret?

I was pleased to see how warm Moxie's dad was to her, and I thought Moxie would be closer to him if it weren't for Martha. Moxie's theory was that Steve never had gotten over the loss of her mother and remarried because he didn't know how to take care of himself and because Moxie needed a mother figure. I personally thought Moxie would have been better off being raised by wolves. But there was something kind in Steve's eyes, and I could tell he truly loved his daughter.

"Everyone, go sit in the living room. I'll bring out something to nosh on while dinner is finishing up."

We all followed each other into the living room and sat awkwardly around a vegetable tray.

"We are very excited to meet you, Michael." Martha placed her hands on her lap.

"It's Miles," Moxie corrected, her voice cold as ice.

"Oh, Miles. I'm so sorry. I thought Moxie said Michael over the phone. Miles is an interesting name. Are you named after someone?

"No, my parents just liked the name," I said, trying to maintain my fake grin.

"Actually, he was found on a pig farm and his parents had to drive miles to get him. Hence the name," Moxie deadpanned. I bowed my head and pressed my lips together to suppress my laughter.

"Moxie, that's not a very nice thing to say. You should apologize." Martha scolded her like a child.

"Martha, you are absolutely right. Miles, would you like me to get on my knees to apologize?"

Martha's mouth hung open and Stephen snickered. I let

out a cough. Damn vixen. I knew she was trying to get a rise out of me and by that, I meant a rise in my pants.

"Are you sure you can handle our Moxie, Miles?" Steve's brows rose as he nodded in Moxie's direction.

"I think she is my perfect balance, Steve. She gets as good as she gives."

"You know, when I was young we would have gotten a spanking if we ever talked like that to someone," Martha said.

"Then you don't know what you're missing," Moxie said back to Martha with a bright smile, batting her eyelashes.

I raised my brow, hopefully conveying that if Moxie kept on being a tease, she would really have to get on her knees to apologize.

Moxie raised her brow back at me, answering that she was fully aware what could be coming her way. I squeezed her knee, my dick hardening just thinking about Moxie on her knees.

"Miles, tell us a little bit about yourself." Martha's voice broke my thoughts, which sent my dick back to hide in its turtle shell.

"Hmm." I thought carefully, not wanting to throw out information that could be used against me later.

"I'm from Maine originally. My parents are still there, but my sister Kelly lives here in Chicago. I have a son Dillion—"

"You have a son? So you've been married before?"

Martha sat up straight.

"Actually, he was probed by aliens and they impregnated him," Moxie said, breaking into the conversation. She took another breath to continue, but I squeezed her knee to calm her.

"Yes, I had previously been married, but my wife was killed in a car accident. Afterward Dillion and I moved to Chicago. Shortly after that I met Moxie; she was Dillion's kindergarten teacher. Dillion loves her." I smiled at Moxie and she beamed. "They're great together."

"I'm sorry to hear about your loss, Miles," Steve injected. "But it sounds like Moxie brought happiness back into your and Dillion's life."

"Yes, sir. She most certainly has." Moxie covered my hand with hers and we interlaced our fingers.

"That's good to hear. I was always concerned that Moxie's work with children would deter her from having children of her own. For a while there we thought she would be a spinster with a herd of cats." Martha laughed, slapping her thigh. However, no one laughed with her.

"Excuse me, I have to go to the bathroom." Moxie shot up from the couch, holding her hand to her mouth, and ran for the bathroom.

"While Moxie is in the bathroom, I'll finish up dinner and we can meet in the dining room. Steve, I need your help in the kitchen."

"Sure," Steve replied stoically.

I walked to the bathroom and tapped on the door. "Moxie? You okay in there?"

"I'm deciding if it's better to throw a body into Lake Michigan or dismember it and bury pieces in different places. However, I was leaning toward kerosene and a match."

"No question, definitely go with the cement slippers and send the body overboard. No one in their right mind would go deep sea fishing in Lake Michigan. Can I come in?"

"No. I'm too busy self-loathing and melting Martha's rose-shaped soap under hot water to look like testicles."

"Good thing you're being productive," I said, chuckling.

The bathroom door opened and Moxie looked flushed. "I vote for telling the baby that it has no grandparents on my side and that I was born through Immaculate Conception."

"Sweet! I always wanted to be married to the Messiah!" Moxie hit me in the shoulder playfully.

"If I'm the Messiah, let's get The Last Supper over with."

Moxie and I entered the dining room and took our seats across from Martha and Steve. The table was filled with things that I think were supposed to resemble food, but was definitely questionable. There was something that looked like potatoes and a green Jell-O mold with fruit in it.

"I make a fantastic brisket, Miles. Everyone who's had it can't wait to take leftovers home with them." Martha beamed.

"Probably to use as mortar to build brick houses," Moxie

said under her breath.

Martha served a heaping amount of "brisket" on top my plate. Moxie took one look at my plate and turned green. This was quickly spiraling out of control. Moxie covered her mouth and pushed the chair back against the wall. She ran out of the room and into the kitchen. We could all hear her emptying the contents of her stomach.

"Moxie!" Martha yelled. "What's wrong? Are you sick? Are you coming down with the flu? Maybe it's a swine flu. Oh God, it's Ebola!"

I heard the sink run and Moxie peeked her head back into the dining room. "We need to go back to the living room. I need to tell you guys something, but it can't be in front of"— she waved her hand over the table—"that."

"Umm, sure, baby girl," Steve said, looking concerned. I wondered about Steve's lack of commentary throughout this evening. The only possible explanation I could think was that Martha wouldn't let him get in a word in edgewise. She always put her two cents in. Or more like a million cents in.

We all resumed our initial seats back in the living room, and I held Moxie's hand for support.

"Moxie, was it the food? I cooked the brisket all day. I know it's your favorite," Martha said.

"I'm pregnant," Moxie blurted out.

You could hear a pin drop. Both Martha and Steve sat in their chairs, looking at us like we told them we created the atomic bomb. Since that wasn't enough of a shock, Moxie added Hiroshima on top of that.

"And we're getting married."

More silence filled the room. I leaned in close to Moxie and whispered, "I don't think you're going to need that cement, I think you just killed her."

"I wouldn't count her out yet. You know what happens when you kill the bad guy in video games?"

"No, what?"

"They come back bigger and stronger for round two."

Finally Martha broke the silence. "Is he Jewish?"

"No, he's not, Martha," Moxie answered before I could.

"How are you going to raise the baby? Where are you going to live?" Martha continued, the hysteria in her voice was starting to rise.

"Martha, I think—"

"No, Steve. Let's hear what they say." Martha crossed her arms and waited.

"Generally, I think if you give it food and change its diaper occasionally, it should be in good shape for a while. But as soon as it becomes a toddler it's going to be survival of the fittest," Moxie said.

"You know what I meant, young lady. How are you going to raise a baby if you are Jewish and he isn't?" Martha pointed her finger at me,

"Oh that's easy," Moxie said. "We're going to raise it Druid."

"Is that a combination of Jewish and something else?" Martha stood up from her chair.

"No, Druids worship trees. There is a nice little pine tree growing in Miles's backyard. We might put some pews around it so we can pray."

I swore a growl came from Martha, and I wondered if I should grab Moxie and duck for cover behind the couch.

"Steve! Say something. Your daughter is pregnant and marrying this Michael person."

"It's Miles!" Moxie yelled, jumping to her feet. I followed suit.

Steve stood out of his recliner and walked over to where Moxie and I were standing. I moved slightly in front of Moxie to protect her from the anything Steve would say to hurt her feelings. But instead he grabbed us both.

"Mazel tov, to you both." He hugged us. "You seem to truly love each other, and I am thrilled to become a grandfather."

Martha stood there for a long time eyeing both Moxie and I. Finally, she moved toward us and plastered on a smile so large that it would have made the Joker jealous.

"I suppose congratulations are in order," she said, her demeanor changing from Snow Bitch to Glenda the Good Witch. "Welcome to the family, Miles."

At that moment, I thought a better phrase would have been "Welcome to the Jungle."

Twelve

Moxie

I knew I was going to get a big reaction from Martha, but I didn't know exactly how it was all going to play out. I figured it was either going to be the start of World War III or she would excuse herself from the meal, go upstairs, and start measuring the guest room to fit a crib. I never knew with Martha. It was like going for sushi. You prayed the fish was fresh, only to find out it wasn't, and you're left sitting on the toilet with explosive diarrhea.

We were able to finish some of the dinner in the living room, keeping Martha's brisket out of sight. I ate my mashed potatoes, because it was the only thing I seemed to tolerate.

We resumed with light conversation and kept clear of all hot button topics which included: Miles not being Jewish, Miles's deceased wife, how we planned on raising our child, and how I was going to fit into a designer wedding dress. I gave Miles the *we served our time, let's get out of here* look.

"Mr. and Mrs. Summers, it was a pleasure meeting you, but Moxie and I need to work tomorrow and we need to get back to Dillion," Miles said politely, standing up and putting our dishes on the coffee table.

"Of course," my dad said as he stood to walk us to the door. "Moxie, it must be reassuring knowing that you're getting some practice with Dillion. He sounds like a great kid."

"He hasn't tried to run away or call Jerry Springer yet, so that's a bonus, I guess," I replied while putting on my coat.

I thought for sure that would spur a comment from Martha, but she was oddly quiet as we reached the door. My dad wrapped me in a hug and shook Miles's hand; a final gesture of welcoming him to the family.

"You seem like a nice guy, Miles. I hope we can get to know each other some more since you're my future son-in-law. We can go out. Golfing, perhaps?"

"I would like that. I'll get your phone number from Moxie and we can set it up. Have a father to soon-to-be son-in-law chat over the links."

"Maybe you can convince him to convert to Judaism." Martha let out a small laugh, and I glared at her murderously. Miles opened the door, letting the cool air into the house. He held his hand to my lower back and guided me out the door.

"I'll walk you to your car," Martha finally jumped in. She grabbed her own coat in a rush and followed us outside. I hoped she would apologize for her outburst earlier. I'm not a golden child, by any means, and she can dish it out to me all she wants, but attack my man and I'll be on you like a crackhead getting her next fix. Minus the crack pipe and missing teeth.

We walked the small path leading from the house to the driveway, and I moaned at my stepmother's clinking heels. "Martha, you didn't have to walk us to the car. Last time I checked I was old enough to walk fifteen feet without guidance."

"I came out here because I need to talk to you without your father around," she said as she looked over her shoulder to make sure Dad hadn't followed us out.

I shot Miles a look and my body tightened, waiting for a shit storm. Too bad I quit karate as a kid. I might need my ninja fighting skills like the Karate Kid. All I remembered was wax on, wax off. But Martha wasn't a car, so that would get me nowhere in this situation.

Getting Martha alone had proven to be dangerous in the past because that's when she was best at manipulating me. The fact she tried to have someone date me so he could convince me to lose weight really put a strain on our relationship. Not that we were tight to begin with. Instead of a small crack in the relationship, it had turned into the Grand Canyon from years of her treatment.

"There is some news that I need to tell you and it's not good." She wrung her hands together and looked at the ground.

I put up my hand to stop her. "Martha, if this is about how your spa consultant took too much hair off your bikini area, I think it can wait. Scratch that, I don't ever want to know."

"Moxie, your father has cancer."

Time froze as soon as Martha said the word *cancer*. An overwhelming feeling of sickness washed over me. The last time I'd heard those words my mom found out she had breast cancer. The time spent in hospitals, chemo sessions, watching her get sicker by the day, finally losing the war, her funeral, strange people offering their condolences, and losing one of the most important people in my life. The memories hit me within those seconds of Martha saying the C word.

"What?" I finally was able to speak. Miles came to my side and put his arm around my waist up for support.

"Your father has cancer and he doesn't want you to know. He found out not long ago, and he thought it would be better if you went about your daily lives and not worry about him," she said, still focusing on the pathway.

"Want kind of cancer?" I heard Miles ask, but it sounded more like an echo speaking from the distance.

Martha paused as if she was already sharing too much information.

"Liver. Doctors aren't sure yet how long he…" She

paused again, but continued, "…has to live."

"Moxie, he doesn't want you to know. You can't say a word to him. It would completely destroy him and I swore I wouldn't say anything."

"But I'm his daughter. Don't you think he knows, seeing as how you followed us outside?" I managed to whisper. Part of me wanted to scream at her about agreeing not to say anything, but I didn't have it within me. Martha and I may have had our issues, but this was also her husband dying.

"No, I told him earlier I was going to invite you and your boyfriend to come to Shabbat dinner. Hopefully, he thinks I'm talking to you about it now. I understand you're hurt, but he's doing it to protect you. The only reason I'm telling you now is because after finding out that you're pregnant and getting married, I thought you might want to make the best memories you could with him in the time he has left."

Tears soaked my cheeks and Miles pulled me closer. "I'm so sorry, sweetness." He kissed my cheek and wiped away the tears with his fingers.

I didn't know how to respond. I had too many receptors firing in my brain and couldn't form words. I was going to lose my dad. Even though I consciously knew all lives would finally end, the thought of losing my dad this soon hurt my heart. Our baby would never get to know her or his grandfather and he wouldn't get to spoil them rotten. I was going to be left without parents at the same time I was going to become a parent myself. I certainly didn't think of Martha as a remaining parent, and I certainly didn't think of her as the sole grandparent from my side of the family.

"Moxie, you have to promise me that you won't say anything. He has to do it his way; it's his dying wish. He'll want to make sure that this wedding and pregnancy go perfect for you because he's going to want you to embrace those memories." She finally lifted her head and swayed from side-to-side. I understood why she looked so nervous; she was going against my dad's wishes.

All I did was nod and buried myself deeper into Miles's body. I craved his comfort because suddenly I felt that he was all that I had left.

"I'm going to take her home, Martha," Miles said. "We can talk about this some more after she's had some time to process it."

"Yes, of course. Moxie, I just want you to remember to make this time the best that it can be and try to give him the most you can before he's gone."

"Thank you, Martha." Miles somehow knew to speak for both of us because I couldn't find the words.

Martha walked back to the house. When she'd followed us out, I was ready to pounce on whatever she was going to say. It was what I was used to doing with her, almost like it was ingrained in me. But I saw something different in the woman walking away. Yes, I was going to lose my father, but she was also going to lose a husband. For better or worse, no one should suffer through the feeling of losing someone you love. I knew in the end we all died. But that didn't lesson the pain when someone was left to grieve for you. It made me look at Martha in a different light. Perhaps, it was going to be a loss that we would weather together.

Miles led me to the car. He opened the passenger seat and kissed my forehead before I slid in. I couldn't tell you how long we'd been driving before I finally realized we'd actually left Martha and my dad's house. My thoughts were a never-ending jumble. Why would he not want me to know? He decided that before he knew I was pregnant and getting married. Did he not think I was strong enough to handle it? Maybe he thought it would be too traumatic for me to know considering what Mom went through.

"I see the wheels in your head turning. What are you thinking?" Miles's question brought me back into the present.

"I guess I just don't understand. Why wouldn't he tell me?" I stared out the windshield.

Miles shrugged. "I'm sure he's trying to protect you. I would do anything to protect Dillion from any sorta pain."

"You wouldn't tell Dillion you were dying?" I looked at him, my eyes brimming with tears.

"I didn't say that. But as a parent you try to protect your children from facing any sort of hurt. Especially if you are the cause of the hurt."

"It must have been hard for Martha to have to tell me about Dad. I know that she was going against his wishes." I looked back out the windshield.

"The jury is still out whether Martha is capable of feeling human emotion."

I smiled and Miles took my hand. "It will be okay. You have me and amazing friends to lean on. We are just as much your family as your dad is."

I supposed that was my one reprieve in this nightmare. I had Miles, Dillion, and this growing human taking up residence at the hotel Summers.

Thirteen

Moxie

I made an emergency phone call to Dr. Gerber the next day and she agreed to see me. She only had morning appointments, so I would have to take the morning off work. I made sure I was armed with tasty treats to eat my anxiety away. I sat in her office and stared at the pale walls, unable to focus on anything but Martha's words from last night.

My dad was dying.

I wasn't naïve to think we are all immortal. I went through Mom's death. But something felt different about this, and I couldn't place what it was. I cried in Miles's arms the night before and he suggested I see Dr. Gerber. He said he would be there to comfort me in anyway, but Dr. Gerber might be better suited to help me process my feelings.

The inner door to her office opened and out stepped Dr. Gerber looking put together and professional, as always. I felt like I was just trampled during the Running of the Bulls. She held the door open and waved me in. I had a favorite part of the couch that I liked to sit on. In my opinion I preferred the squishy end as opposed to worn end where everyone else poured out their dark souls. Dr. Gerber took her place in her chair, crossed her legs, and just waited.

"You're not going to say 'Good morning' or 'How was the traffic?' "

She drew in a breath through her nose and clasped her hands over her knees. "I figured when I got an emergency call that the usual pleasantries are probably not needed.

"So you're going to sit there and stare at me?"

"No, I'm going to wait until you're ready to talk. There's no rush. Well, besides the fact that you have fifty-two minutes left of your session." She winked.

It was the simple gesture of a wink that helped me relax. I've come to like Dr. Gerber. She wasn't patronizing and didn't blame everything on Freud's theory that everyone just wanted to suck on their mother's tits… or something.

"My dad is dying," I said softly.

"I'm so sorry, Moxie," she replied, warmth wrapping her words.

"The weird thing is that I have all different feelings and emotions swirling in my head. I can't just catch one and deal with it."

"We've talked a little about your family, mostly about Martha. But what is your relationship with your dad like?"

I told Dr. Gerber about my dad and she listened without interruption. I loved my dad, and the thought of losing him left a part of me empty. I had a lot of memories of my dad playing with me as a kid and how he always spoiled me rotten. But when my mom died, things changed for him. Even after meeting Martha, his personality never matched what it had been before mom passed.

"So do you think Martha changed him?"

"No, I think he was broken after my mom. We never really spoke about his remarriage. Instead I just acted out toward Martha. She was easier to blame than my dad."

"Why did you want to blame him?" she asked.

Tears formed in my eyes as years of pain surfaced. I blame my dad—blame him for essentially leaving me, mentally. Sure he was physically there, but part of him was buried with my mom. I wanted to blame him for this woman he brought into our lives. I wanted to blame him because I needed him to soothe away my grief, not give me a makeshift mommy. I blurted this all and other word vomit, everything from Martha telling me he didn't want me to know to my dad wanting me to have a perfect wedding.

"So where does Martha fit into all of this?"

I took a deep breath and pondered that question before answering. "When I looked at Martha after she told me, I saw a flash of a different woman. It was a woman who was going to lose her husband. I can't even think about what would happen if I lost Miles. She still bugs the ever living shit out of me. But I'm willing to deal with my feelings for her if that will make my dad happy."

"Why is it so important now for you to make your dad happy? You just gave me a list of reasons you blame him."

I looked at Dr. Gerber with narrowed eyes. Why was it so important now? Why was I willing to put up with Martha's shit all of a sudden? I took a tissue from the side table and dried my eyes. Then it hit me. I sat up and looked at the woman who'd just helped me turn the lights on.

"Because through everything—the good, bad, and ugly— he's still my dad. He's still the man who had tea parties with me and my bears when I was seven. He's still the man who bought me a red velvet dress I refused to take off for two days when I was eight. And he's still the man who will proudly walk me down the aisle to the other man who loves me just as fiercely."

Dr. Gerber's lips curled into a smile. "Congratulations, Moxie."

"For what?" I asked, while patting the snot dripping from my nose.

"Because now, we're finally getting somewhere."

Fourteen

Miles

I stood in the shower, letting the water massage my back. The water was so hot it was burning my skin, but it felt good. But I seriously contemplated turning the knob to cold and dousing my raging hard-on. It had been almost four months since Moxie had told me she was pregnant and we had that amazing sex at Disney World. Since then the morning sickness, fatigue, and worries about her dad had replaced any desire she had to make love.

I stared down at the erection I'd been sporting since I watched Moxie get ready for bed tonight. The way she peeled off her clothes piece by piece, I could have sworn she knew she was torturing me. I closed my eyes and replayed the scene in my head. She sauntered into the room and stretched her arms over her head, pushing her tits out as if it were an invitation. Her V-neck sweater stretched tight across her chest and I ached to touch what was underneath. When she did, she revealed her plump breasts in a purple lace bra. The pregnancy had made her already sizable breasts even bigger. My cock pounded with need with the thought of moving it in and out of those tits, fucking them until I came.

My misery didn't end there. Moxie lowered her jeans to reveal matching purple panties. Her red locks fell over her shoulders as she bent to take each pant leg off. I desperately wanted to grab her from behind and show her exactly how I felt about her unintentional strip tease. The visual of her bent over while I took her from behind was enough to make me lose my breath.

I seriously needed to find release. I grabbed the bar of soap and rubbed it in between my hands to create a foaming lather. I gripped my cock, which was achingly hard and slid over the shaft with my soapy hand. A hard breath escaped my lips as the suds lubed my skin. Slowly, I pumped my shaft, stopping for a second to grip the tip. The tip of my dick was always the most sensitive. Moxie's little party trick was to take her finger and slowly play with the slit on the head. My breathing picked up as well as the movement of my hand.

"You know, I should feel insulted."

I startled and released my cock. I wiped away the condensation building on the shower glass door. Moxie stood in nothing but one of my button down dress shirts.

"Feeling a little physically frustrated?" she asked in a sultry voice, which was not helping my cause. My poor cock was going to explode.

"If it makes you feel any better, I was thinking about you." I threw Moxie a wry smile.

"Oh yeah? And what were you thinking exactly?" Moxie slid the shower door open, letting the cool air from the room into the shower. I thought the coolness would shrink my erection, but looking at my girl in my shirt just made my cock throb even more.

"I was thinking about your sweet ass and taking you from behind." I couldn't help it; I took my dick back into my hand and started stroking it again.

"Hmm, that sounds kind of dull." She faked a yawn and patted her mouth with her hand.

I raised an eyebrow, still trying to fight my desire for her. But a man can only take so much. I grabbed her arm, pulling her into the shower with me, my dress shirt getting drenched. The wet material of the shirt clung to her body. Her nipples clearly were hard, screaming to be released from the shirt. And who was I to deny them their request? I took the front of the shirt and ripped it open, sending the buttons across the shower floor.

"Now look at what you did. I liked this shirt." Moxie pouted.

"I liked it too, but it was in the way of what I wanted."

"And what's that?"

"These," I said, taking a breast in each hand.

Moxie let out a small cry and I paused for a moment remembering back when we were at Disney when she said they were painful to touch. Dear God, I hoped that wasn't the case anymore because I missed them.

"They are so sensitive now," she said. "I read that they can get super sensitive with the pregnancy. But not like before, now it feels amazing."

With that being said, I massaged her nipples with the palms of my hands. Moxie always loved when I played with her nipples.

"Oh God, Miles."

"Feel good?" I asked, knowing the answer because her hips bucked toward me.

"You have no idea," she said and purred through her pleasure.

I continued my onslaught of her breasts by rolling each nipple in between my fingers.

Moxie braced herself on the wall and glass door to keep from falling over. She panted, "Miles, I can't… the feeling… too intense."

I stopped kneading her nipples and clutched her hips. I scrutinized her face and looked for signs that I should stop, but all I saw was passion and lust. I took that as a green light to continue and pressed my lips to hers. I was greedy and hungry and wanted nothing more than to be with her. She broke the kiss and looked at me.

"I think I owe you for being so patient with me while I moved past the first trimester crap."

"You don't owe me anything, I have all I could want." I cupped her cheek.

"Everything?" She smiled.

"Well, there is one thing."

"That would be?"

"You… on your knees… sucking me off."

"Your wish is my command."

She slowly sunk to her knees, scratching her nails down my stomach as she went. My cock jutted out in front of me, pointing directly at her mouth and begging to be devoured. She licked across my shaft. My head fell back and my eyes rolled back in my head. Moxie opened her mouth and took me in all the way, her head bobbing back and forth, sucking me with intensity. I automatically reached for her hair and tangled my fingers in her red mane.

"Take me in, sweetness. As far as you can go."

Moxie hummed while sucking me, sending even more waves of pleasure through me. I had to stop her or else I was going to come and I desperately wanted to come inside of her.

"I need you to stop," I said, stilling her head. Her pleading eyes looked up to me and she made a popping sound when she released my cock from her sweet lips.

"Something wrong? Did you not like it?" She ran her tongue over her lips.

She knew I loved it when she blew me, so I wasn't going to respond to that. "I want you bent over the shower bench. I'll show you exactly what I was thinking about while I was jerking off."

"Knowing your dirty mind, it could have been a million different scenarios."

I helped Moxie up, spun her around, and slowly pushed her back down so she was bent over, holding onto the edge of the bench. Her ass sticking up was an invitation. I brought my hand through her opened thighs and found her opening and shoved two fingers into her heat and stroked her clit with my thumb.

"Is my sweetness ready for me?

"Yes," Moxie huffed out.

"Mmm, I can tell by how fucking wet you are."

It took everything to restrain myself from plowing into her. But I had to admit that teasing Moxie was also a huge turn-on for me. Just watching her struggle with desire, spurred me on.

"Miles, please. I need you now."

"What do you need, Moxie?

I knew exactly what she needed. In the time I'd been with her I'd gotten to know Moxie's body as well as my own. I knew what drove her mad and what made her sing with pleasure.

"I need you to fuck me."

"Do you want me to fuck you soft and sweet or hard and fast?"

"Hard. Now."

"Your wish is my command," I said, repeating her earlier saying.

With a swift thrust I entered her and held onto her hips. Moxie sucked in air like she was fighting to breathe. "It's going to be fast, sweetness. I've needed this for too long."

"God, Miles. I love it when you take me."

I continued to pound into her, my intensity only growing more as I moved. My hand left her hip and reached around and rubbed her clit. I bent down to kiss her between her shoulder blades. "Come for me, Moxie. Come on my cock."

I knew that's all it would take and felt her body shutter and her pussy clenched around my cock like a vise. I moved faster, sending both of us to the edge.

"Now, Moxie, fucking come now."

Moxie screamed as her orgasm took over her body. I felt a roll start in my lower spine and rose until I poured myself into the woman I loved so much. After a few minutes, we both came down from the orgasmic high. She straightened herself and I wrapped my arms around her, pressing kisses on her neck.

"I missed you," I whispered into her ear. She turned around. Her eyes were closed and she had a small, closed smile on her lips. I wanted to hold her forever and feel her heartbeat next to mine.

"I know. I missed you, too." She shifted until she nested it into the crook of my neck.

"I take it you're feeling better?" I reached down and rubbed small circles around her stomach. She giggled, backing away slightly and gently swatted my hand away.

"Yeah, I think your spawn is finally releasing me from vomiting purgatory."

"Good. My spawn knows that Daddy needs Mommy's pussy."

"Never, and I mean ever, say Mommy's pussy again," she said, as she looked me straight into my eyes and pointed a stern finger at me.

I laughed, turned off the shower, and opened the door to get a towel. I swung the soft towel around Moxie first, drying every inch from head to toe. I stopped briefly, at her abdomen and bent down to give it a kiss.

"Hey, sprout. I love your mommy very much. And I especially like her when she's bent over in the shower."

Moxie went to smack my arm, but I guarded myself before she could get to me. There wasn't enough words to express how I felt about this woman and the life growing inside her. Working with Dr. Gerber was definitely helping Moxie overcome some of her fears about becoming a mother and I could see her confidence growing.

"I swear our baby is going to come out spewing obscenities since its father is such a dirty talker," she said as she ran her fingers over my lips.

"Umm, last time I checked, its mother's mouth lived permanently in the gutter."

"I don't know what you're talking about, you pussy-loving butt slave."

"Butt slave?"

"Yeah. Because you're a slave to my ass, so you're my butt slave."

"Sweetness, when you're no longer on this earth, I shall make a shrine of your voluptuous ass and I'll kiss it every damn day."

Fifteen

Moxie

Renee, Ryan, and I were sitting at The Cheesecake Factory on Michigan Avenue having lunch and looking at bridal magazines. It was still surreal for me as we turned the pages, looking at all the women draped in white taffeta. Well, mostly white. There was a bright red dress perfect for a hooker's wedding. Hey, I don't judge. Too much.

"When I was younger, I would sit in the magazine aisle at the grocery store looking at wedding dresses while my mom went shopping." Renee sighed as she flipped through the pages.

"Wouldn't she worry that you would get abducted if you weren't near her at all times?"

Ryan raised a brow.

"I thought parents plaster their kids to their hips so that Steve the Stranger doesn't lure them with a piece of candy into their conversion vans."

"Nah. My mom figured if a stranger came up to me, I would talk their ear off and they would beg my parents to take me back," she said, not even looking away from the pages.

I looked at Ryan and shrugged. Renee did have a tendency to yammer on. When it came down to safety, Renee had the upper hand. A little hidden tidbit about Renee was that she had a black belt in Tae Kwon Do. Her dad was a police officer and made sure she knew how to protect herself. I found out this information one night when a guy at a bar got a little too handsy with Renee on the dance floor. He only needed fifteen stitches and still had vision in his left eye. Renee said she went easy on him.

The waitress came over to take our order and brightened when she saw the mess of magazines in front of us.

"Oh, who's getting married?" she asked, beaming with excitement. The look around the table for a viable option. She looked at Renee with a big toothy grin as if she had found the answer.

"I am," I said as I lifted one hand and rested the other on my ever-growing abdomen.

"Oh." The waitress sounded disappointed as she looked me over and narrowed her eyes, her lips drawn in a thin line.

"My partner here and I are finally taking the plunge." I grabbed Renee's hand. The waitress quickly looked at Renee and me and sputtered her apologies. I waved her off and continued because it was too fun.

"And this is our baby daddy, Phil. He was generous enough to donate his sperm so we could have kids." Then I lowered my voice so only the four of us could hear. "But I had to fuck him since the she was using the turkey baster for our Thanksgiving dinner. Shh," I said, placing my finger on my lips.

"Umm, that's very nice," The waitress said, unable to meet my eyes.

"Can you give us a few minutes?" Renee asked the waitress.

As the waitress walked away Renee gave me her best stern teacher eyes. The kind you give a student when you know they did something they weren't supposed to, but didn't have the energy to reprimand them verbally.

"What?" I asked.

"I'm pissed."

"Why? The waitress was being bitchy and I'm hormonal."

"Why did you have to have sex with Ryan when I'm sure there are plenty of professional fertility treatment centers where we could have conceived our child? And the waitress wasn't bitchy, you are just hormonal."

Ryan and I looked at each other in confusion and then back at Renee.

"You do know it was all made up, right? You and I aren't lesbians and we are not having Ryan's baby."

"I just don't understand why I wouldn't be able to have a say in the creation of our child. And why am I cooking Thanksgiving dinner. You know I hate to cook." Renee groaned and shook her head, returning her attention back to the magazine.

"Umm, something on your mind Renee?" Ryan asked.

She slapped the magazine shut and folded her arms.

"I just don't understand why someone else always gets to make decisions for me. I have a voice, a mind, and opinion. I deserve to be heard."

"If it matters to you that much, I'll let you choose the type of cheesecake we'll have for dessert," Ryan offered.

I slapped Ryan's arm. "There's more to it, you dick licker. And what the hell is the matter with you? I'm pregnant, therefore I get to choose the cheesecake and it's going to be Snickers. Now Renee, can you please tell us what has your thong in a twist?"

"Raj said he and I are moving in together. There was no discussion about it or where we'd live. It was just... 'You move here, woman,' " she said in a caveman voice while pointing to the ground.' "

"I thought that's what you wanted?" I opened my menu.

"It is. But I'd like to have some input, not just be told that it's going to happen. I feel like he's trying to be a father to me."

"You did tell me that the other night in bed you called Raj Big Daddy." I smiled.

Ryan almost busted his gut laughing.

Renee's response was something one of her fifth grade students would salute her with—the bird.

"Okay, back to business. We only have a short time to eat before our appointment at the bridal salon, and you have to start pinning down some ideas," Ryan said as he took the menu from me and replaced it with a magazine.

"I have a better idea. Why don't we have a barn themed wedding and I can get married in overalls. The cows can be my bridesmaids and roosters can be groomsmen."

"While I always enjoy a nice cock next to me, I think it would be better to keep things more traditional," Ryan added.

After we ordered and ate, we rounded out our meal with a not so healthy slice of Snickers cheesecake. I tried to convince Renee we shouldn't leave the waitress a low tip because she rubbed me the wrong way. But Renee said something about karma and she didn't want the baby coming out with three heads if we stiffed her and that I was being overly hormonal. I loved my best friend, but she was the most superstitious person I knew. Once she dropped her compact case on the floor, breaking the mirror inside. She cried for two hours, swearing that she was doomed to seven years of bad luck. To ward off the bad luck, she took a whole can of salt and poured it over her shoulder. Too bad it was the wrong shoulder, but I didn't tell her that.

We walked to the bridal salon on an upscale street of Chicago. Martha said my dad wanted to pay for the very best dress available. Who was I to reject the idea of a designer wedding dress? Although at this point in my pregnancy I would be happy to get married in sweatpants and a T-shirt.

We made it to a small building that had beautiful wedding dresses displayed in the large window. All of the samples looked like they wouldn't fit a woman over a size two. I was sure that a dress for larger women or pregnant women wouldn't draw in the correct clientele if they were placed next to the petite ones in the window. Inside, the beautiful boutique looked like something out of Barbie's dream house. Pastel pink wallpaper covered the walls and crystal chandeliers hung from the ceiling. The smell of lilac candles burning was overpowering. There were three-way mirrors positioned in front of couches where friends and family could sit and view the bride as she modeled all the dresses in front of them.

A woman dressed in a black pencil skirt, crème silk blouse walked up to us.

"Hello, may I assist you?"

"Yes, I am here to try on some wedding dresses," I said.

"Oh, that's phenomenal! My name is Sandy. Do you have an appointment scheduled?" Sandy strode to the desk and opened the appointment book.

"It's under Moxie Summers."

"What a fantastic name. We will definitely have to find a dress that lives up to that."

I instantly liked Sandy, even with her sophisticated appearance, she still had a vibrant personality, which made me feel a little more at ease about the situation. Wedding dress shopping was unnerving when you're pregnant and don't want to feel judged.

Sandy came back to us from the desk. "Are you expecting another person?"

"Umm, nope. Just us." I waved my hand toward Ryan and Renee.

"Because I got a phone call yesterday asking when the Summers party would be coming in."

I gave Sandy a puzzled look. Who could be calling to ask when I was coming dress shopping? Miles? That seemed out of place considering I told Miles if he saw my dress before the wedding I would take his balls and place them in his eye sockets so he couldn't see. Before I could ask Sandy if the phone call came from a man or a woman, the door to the boutique swung open, and I nearly lost the Snickers cheesecake I had eaten.

Martha.

"What the hell are you doing here?" I clenched my teeth so hard, I was convinced that I would break some.

"I couldn't miss my daughter trying on wedding gowns.

This is every mother's dream!"

Sandy clapped her hands together. "Oh, that is so beautiful—"

"Martha, you are my stepmother and I wanted this time to be with my friends."

"I'm here for your father. He wasn't feeling good and wanted to make sure that you found your dream dress. I couldn't say no to him because this wedding means so much to him. This could be the last time we all share a special occasion as large as this."

I felt a pounding in my chest as if my heart had broken into pieces. I thought about my dad walking me down the aisle, knowing how proud he would be of me and the woman I had become. I didn't have the heart to let him down, even if it meant I had to deal with Martha.

Ryan came up behind me and whispered, "I say we take one of the dresses, wrap it around her head, and run for the hills. Don't worry, I'll use that ugly dress in the corner."

"That's really kind of you to suffocate my stepmonster, and I have thought about the idea on a number of occasions, but I'm doing this for my dad."

Ryan massaged my shoulders to relieve the stress, but it was a failed attempt.

"Why don't we move into one of the dressing suites, and I can start pulling some dresses to look at. What are you looking for, Moxie?" Sandy asked.

"I think a ball gown that sweeps to the floor would be simply majestic," Martha added.

"Martha, you do know that I will be showing when this takes place, right?" I looked at her like she was smoking crack.

"I thought this would be a beautiful way to accent the joy that was coming to your life," Martha said with a rueful smile.

I turned to Sandy. "I was thinking of something tea length. Perhaps a capped shoulder and definitely with some room to grow." I put my hands on my stomach and looked down at my baby bump.

"I have a few ideas that I can pull. Why don't you all have a seat and relax. Can I bring out some champagne?" Ryan and Renee both raised their hands in unison. I grumbled with jealousy. "I'll just take a glass of water, thanks."

"Of course." Sandy smiled and left the four of us sitting in the dressing room. To say that there was an uncomfortable silence in the room would have been an understatement. But Martha, being Martha, was quick to start talking.

"I have fantastic news," she said.

"You have a meeting you forgot about and have to leave?" Ryan replied.

"Oh, Ryan. You're such a jokester. I remember when you pretended to be straight and brought Moxie to her cousin's wedding. I knew something was up when you pinched one of the groomsmen's tushies."

I put a hand on Ryan's arm, holding back his reply, and

simply shook my head.

"I have an appointment for us to meet with the best wedding coordinator in Chicago after this appointment." She clapped her hands and bounced up and down in her seat.

"Umm, wow. That's… nice," I said. I already had an appointment scheduled with a coordinator that Miles and I had picked. I spoke to her on the phone and she had a good idea of what we wanted.

Sandy came back into the room carrying massive gown bags behind her. An assistant came in after her holding a tray of champagne and water.

"I knew exactly what dresses to pull when you described them to me. We have a section of maternity dresses and I think we will be able to find the perfect dress. I also pulled some that your mom wanted to see on you as well."

"She's my stepmom," I pointed out.

"Let's try on hers first, and I want to save my favorite for last," Sandy said with a sparkle in her eye.

Sandy hung the dresses and unzipped the first garment bag. Tulle poured out and my stomach sank. Sure, as a child I would have loved a big puffy, Cinderella dress. But my style had changed and since I was pregnant I had other ideas in mind.

Our mouths fell open as we looked at the gown Sandy pulled out of the bag. The bust was surrounded by crystals and tiny buttons ran from the back of the dress down the train, which had to be ten feet long. I felt sick; the dress was hideous.

"That is stunning!" Martha said with glee. "You must try it on, Moxie."

I looked at Ryan and Renee, trying to mentally to ask them to shoot me now. Ryan stepped out while I undressed and put on the monstrosity of the dress. It took Renee, Martha, Sandy, and her assistant to get me into the dress. I could only imagine what it would take when I was seven to eight months pregnant. We would need a giant shoe horn. After it was finally on, Ryan came back into the room and started laughing hysterically.

"Moxie, your dad would be so happy with this dress. It's perfect."

"Martha, it looks like the Stay Puft Marshmallow Man came over and took a dump on me."

"Watch your mouth, young lady. It's perfect in every way." She clasped her hands together.

"We have more to try on, so why don't we get out of this one and try on the others?" My head dipped forward and I groaned. After the marshmallow diarrhea dress, I tried on several more that I didn't think were "the one," but then Sandy unzipped the last bag and pulled out a stunning, white, tea length dress. It had a satin top lace, three quarter inch sleeves and a chiffon shirt that flowed to my knees. The finishing touch was a white ribbon that tied in the back. There were dainty, lace cap sleeves that completed the look of the dress. It was perfect because it was elegant and allowed plenty of space for my pregnant belly. I knew it was the one even before I tried it on.

Ryan and Renee gasped when they saw the dress. This was the vision I had in my mind. Sandy helped me step into the dress and closed up the back, tying the bow in place. I turned to see myself in the mirror. Some have said that every girl will have that moment when she will see herself in the mirror with the perfect wedding dress and will start to cry. The feelings will overwhelm her so much, she'll become emotional. I looked at Martha to see her reaction to the dress I loved. She curled her lips with icy contempt, but I ignored her.

I turned around to everyone else in the room and said, "We have a winner, bitches!"

Sixteen

Moxie

After Sandy took some measurements, Martha put a down payment on the dress. We then left to meet Martha's wedding coordinator. I was beyond thankful Renee and Ryan were with me because I needed backup. Miles and I had discussed what we wanted for the wedding and we were on the same page about everything until I suggested we all wear overalls and roast a pig in the backyard. I was kidding, of course, but not the part about roasting the pig. Maybe I would accidentally push Martha into the fire pit with an apple placed firmly in her mouth.

The wedding coordinator's office wasn't that far from the

bridal boutique so we walked over instead of hailing a cab. The office was located in a new building that had replaced one of the original structures in the area. It looked completely out of place with the rest of the architecture around it. It was sleek and white on the outside with round windows that surrounded every level. The door frame of the building was lopsided and looked like something out of a Tim Burton movie. Burton films scared the shit out of me and I was convinced I was going to have nightmares.

"I hope they don't coordinate weddings that look like this building. I'm afraid Beetlejuice will be the officiant marrying us." I looked at the contemporary art pieces that filled the lobby.

"That is your one time to say that." Renee looked at me with wide eyes.

"What? Beetlejuice?"

"Shhh! He will appear if you say it three times," she whispered.

Ryan's lips curved at the corner and one eyebrow shot up. Renee could be a little neurotic.

"No, it's true. I was at a sleepover once and one of the girls said it three times and then he jumped out at us."

"I thought you told me once that it was her younger brother trying to freak you out." I rolled my eyes at Renee's absurdity.

"It doesn't matter! If you say it three times, bad things will happen." She wrapped her arms defensively around her midsection.

I walked up to Renee and stood nose to nose with her and quietly whispered, "Beetlejuuuuice."

"Well, helloooo, everyone!" The owner of the shrill voice, a woman with teased, brown hair and a leopard print dress, walked in our direction.

I turned back to Renee and wrapped my arms around her shoulders in terror. "You were right! I'm sorry I didn't listen. Make the evil monster go away!"

"Who is the lucky bride?" The scary leopard print woman asked.

I pointed to Ryan while he pointed at me. I could only imagine what this lady's ideas for my wedding were going to include. Visions of plates heaping of cheese cubes doled out by people with hair nets. Gaudy neon hearts, papier–mâché… Was there a Moose Lodge in the area? She probably already had it reserved for us. Granted, I shouldn't have judged a book by its cover, but the cover screamed tacky so it was pretty hard to ignore.

Martha grabbed my arm and pulled me forward. "This is the blushing bride, her name is Moxie. And I'm her mother, Martha."

"Actually, stepmom, Martha," I said.

"It's fantastic to meet you both, I'm Julie, your wedding coordinator."

Wait, back the farm tractor up. I didn't remember signing

any paperwork that we were working with this tragedy of a woman. I narrowed my eyes at Martha, sensing she had something to do to with the decision making process.

"Julie is the best in the field," Martha said, trying to defend her actions. "Plus your dad wanted you to have the best wedding. He actually suggested we use her."

"How would my dad know anything about wedding coordinators?" I asked.

"He looked it up on the Internet," Martha replied.

I thought this piece of information was suspicious considering that my dad didn't even know how to use the Internet. But I decided to store this piece of information away because I wanted to make him happy. He probably told Martha he wanted the best and Martha helped him navigate his way around the web.

"And who are these two darling people?" Julie waved to Ryan and Renee.

"They're my bodyguards," I responded before Renee and Ryan got the chance to talk.

"They look pretty small and thin to be bodyguards," Julie said, eyeing them both up and down.

"Trust me, they might be small, but they're scrappy. Especially this one." I pointed to Renee. "She does this thing where she bends down to your feet and bites your ankles. Three people are bound to wheelchairs for life because of her."

Renee and Ryan giggled behind me.

"She's such a jokester." Martha gave me a disapproving look. "That is Renee and Ryan. They are the maid of honor and best man."

"Okay, well then, shall we get started? My office is this way if you'd like to follow me."

The four of us followed Julie into her large office. The room was decorated with examples of different wedding paraphernalia: centerpieces, fake cakes, wedding invitations, and dear God... there were neon hearts. I think I actually heard Ryan's jaw fall to the floor in disgust. Ryan was a huge fan of the show *My Fair Wedding*. And took it upon himself to know what was tasteful and god-awful when it came to wedding planning. So for Ryan, this was stepping into hell.

"Why don't you all have a seat at the table, and I'll pull out my portfolio to share some of the past weddings I've done," Julie said as she moved one of the fake cakes with little stairs connecting the three tiers.

Renee leaned over to whisper in my ear. "How much do you want to bet that she's only done weddings for the mafia?"

"If that's true, I'm surprised they didn't give her a cement bath and throw her into the Chicago River because it was so awful."

Julie returned with her overstuffed portfolio. Thumbing through the pages of her portfolio, I was stunned by the beautiful weddings she had planned. Maybe I didn't give her enough credit or maybe I was hallucinating.

"Before we begin, Moxie, why don't you tell me what you

imagine your dream wedding to look like," Julie asked while opening up her large notepad.

"My fiancé and I have talked about having the wedding around June. I know that's quick, but we didn't want to wait for the end of the pregnancy."

Martha let out a little cough.

"Yes, Martha?" I said with annoyance.

"I think your father would like to have a late summer early fall wedding."

"Does he realize I'll be as big as a house by then, and he'll have to roll me down the aisle?"

"I know, sweetie, but I'm just stating what your father wants."

I rolled my eyes, realizing that this appointment was going to be a struggle if Martha kept this crap up. I just had to keep reminding myself that it was for Dad. I knew it was not Dad's wedding, but I wanted to do as much as I could to make him happy in the time he had left. Even having Martha around, I never saw that same sparkle in his eye. I hoped that having this celebration would put that bit of happiness back in his soul before he passed on. Tearing up, I a grabbed a tissue from the box that sat on the table.

"Oh honey, are you okay?" Renee asked and took my free hand.

"Yeah, pregnancy hormones and the idea of finally getting married." I lied.

Whenever I told Julie what Miles and I wanted, Martha was there at every turn contradicting every suggestion. I said that we wanted to keep it relatively small, and Martha reminded me we had to invite all the extended family because they would have invited us. I said we didn't want black tie and Martha insisted on a formal gathering. Through all of this there was one demand I wasn't going to budge on.

"Julie, in a Jewish wedding we have a chuppah. It's like a canopy that covers the bride and groom during the service. My dad's sister is taking my mom's wedding dress and creating the cloth that will hang above us. It's very important to me that this be included in the wedding."

"Moxie, if I would have known that I would have given you pieces of the suit I wore when I married your dad. It could have been a symbol of your two mothers," Martha said.

In unison Renee and Ryan grabbed my arms. They knew I would go all Kung Foo on her ass. I only had nine years with my mom and part of me always felt she was watching over me. When I made good choices, she celebrated with me. When I made bad choices, she shook her angelic head and closed her eyes. There was no way Martha would ever take that precious time away from me. The chuppah was a symbol that represented my mom watching me make the best decision of my life: marrying Miles.

I gathered every ounce of patience I had left. "Martha, having my mom's dress is a symbol of my past. It's important to me to have that there."

"I am part of your past, too." She huffed as she repositioned herself in her chair.

"Breathe, Moxie. Let's practice Lamaze. Hee, hee, hooo. Hee, hee, hooo," Renee said quietly in my ear.

"Moving on," I said to the group.

"Okay, let's talk about the cake." Julie opened a massive binder with designs for just cakes. My mouth salivated knowing that there was confectionary goodness within my grasp. I didn't want a traditional cake; I wanted cupcakes. I had a deep-seated love affair with cupcakes. The perfect cupcake was like a flawless blow job. A cupcake was a perfect-sized dessert that could slip into your mouth with ease; velvety cake mixed with creamy frosting that glided down your throat. Julie started to flip through the pages one by one as she talked about the different flavors and the difference between frostings. Did we want fondant, whip cream, or buttercream? Martha stopped Julie from flipping to the next page.

"This is perfect!" Martha took the book out of Julie's hands. It was a three tiered cake that had little plastic staircases which led down to two smaller cakes. Plastic doves sat on top of the cake and two small water fountains sat next to the two smaller cakes.

Ryan started roaring with laughter. "Martha, I didn't realize that you had such a great sense of humor."

Martha scowled. "Ryan, just because you're gay doesn't mean you have perfect design sense when it comes to weddings. And now that Illinois allows gay marriages, you can pick out your own cake."

Oh. Fucking. No.

"Martha, that was totally out of line," I said, trying to keep my anger at bay. Ryan started getting out of his seat, but I held his knee down with my hand under the table and shook my head at him. There was no way he was leaving me now.

"Martha, how did the cake taste at your wedding? I bet it tasted light and airy. Oh, I forgot, there was no cake at your wedding." Ryan crossed his arms across his chest and looked only half satisfied at his rebuttal.

"That was because we got married in the Rabbi's office. Moxie's dad wants to give her want we didn't have."

"I don't think you're dad wanted to give you a conniving bitch for your wedding like he ended up with," Ryan said to only me as he pretended to bend down and tie his shoe.

"No, instead I got a T-shirt that said, my dad got married and all I got was this lousy snatch for a stepmom," I whispered back. I tried hard to remember the woman I saw after she told me Dad was dying, but Martha made it almost impossible to warm up to her, especially when she insulted my friends.

At least that gave Ryan a little giggle to warm his mood. The five of us talked for another hour with Martha interjecting at every suggestion I made. Finally, I gave up and said that it was all fine with the exception of my dress, the chuppah, and the cupcakes. Those were the three things that mattered to me most. For a moment I felt a little bad that Martha never had a cake, but then I remembered how she treated Ryan. I'll have a special cupcake made just for her—with rat poison frosting.

The Pregnancy Guide

Months 5 and 6

Women

Worried about what the scale says? Don't! Your baby is growing and so are you. Some woman start to gain about a pound a week. Good nutrition is always an important part during your pregnancy. You know that old saying that you're eating for two? It's true! Eating correctly will help your baby grow strong. Are those pet commercials making you cry? Don't worry, this is normal. Women become more emotional during their pregnancy and often cry at the drop of a hat. Just remember that you are loved and so is the life growing inside you. One of the most exciting things is that you are able to find out the gender of your baby!

Men

You might be thinking, "Dear God, what is that thing growing out of our partner's ass?" It's a fucking hemorrhoid, not the baby's head. You better workout because you're going to need it. She'll ask you to rub her legs and ass because of leg cramps and sciatica pain. The water works will also get worse. The cool part? You can find out if you're having a boy or a girl. That's right, you can see if your little man is hung like a horse or if you'll need to buy a gun because no one will be dating your daughter.

Seventeen

Moxie

The bedroom had turned into a scene from the show *Hoarders*. Clothes were scattered everywhere. I lay in the middle of the bed surrounded by pants, shirts and dresses, all of which were too snug on me. I could no longer get away with leaving my pants unbuttoned. This couldn't have come at a worst time. Miles had decided it was time I met his parents. His mom and dad were coming from Maine to meet their soon-to-be daughter-in-law, or as I would have liked to phrase it, the Baby Mama.

It wasn't like I was a complete phantom to Mr. And Mrs. Dane. They'd known about me since Miles had started dating me, but I didn't think they were expecting us to be pregnant and getting married so soon. Well, to be fair, I didn't think any of us thought that was going to happen. I already had a good relationship with his sister, Kelly, but there was something daunting about meeting your fiancé's parents for the first time. Or in this case, I would say my Baby Daddy's parents. So would that make them the baby grandparents? Maybe I just could call them the baby Gs.

There was only one person who could help me in such a crisis. I found my phone and sent a text to my fashion consultant, Ryan.

What's up, blue balls?

You know, it's not fair to make fun of my aching balls since I am without a boyfriend.

But God gave you a permanent boyfriend called your hand.

We're not on speaking terms right now. I caught my finger in a drawer the other day, now have a nice scrape and bruise.

I really needed to take Ryan out to look for a man. He deserved happiness and just talking about his own balls wasn't as fun as talking about him and someone else's balls. The more balls you had in a conversation, the better.

You know that's boyfriend abuse, right?

Did you text me to taunt me over my masturbation ethics or did you actually have a real purpose?

I have bad news.

CAROL CHANNING DIED???

Oh my God. Ryan needed to tone the gay down a notch.

> *Isn't she already dead? Anyways, none of my clothes fit, and I'm meeting Miles's parents. Are you up for a shopping trip?*

> *OMG, can we go to A Pea in the Pod and strap one of those pillows to your stomach to see what clothes you can wear at eight months?*

Just going to a place called A Pea in the Pod made me cringe, but I was going to suck it up. It would look a little strange being nine months pregnant with size sixteen jeans pasted on.

> *If you make me look eight months on purpose, I will detach your balls and make you swallow them.*

> *Okay, perhaps a few items for you to get by.*

> *Meet me at the mall at eleven.*

> *See you then.*

I put on a pair of yoga pants and a long T-shirt, the last of my clothing that fit. I didn't do yoga, but Miles had a certain affinity for how I looked in yoga pants so I bought several pairs. I was thankful that I did because it was the only thing willing to make room for my expanding belly.

"I'm going to start charging you rent," I said to my stomach. "It's better to learn financial responsibly at a young age. You'd better start saving up."

I had some time before I met Ryan at the mall, so I stepped around the forest of clothes and went into the family room. I was still attending weekly sessions with Dr. Gerber, but hadn't written a single letter to mini me. I figured if I was starting to have conversations with my stomach, now would be a good time to start writing to it as well. I sat on the couch and took the pad of paper and pencil that was sitting on the coffee table.

Dear It,

This is your mother.

I paused and looked at the word mother. Holy fucking shitballs, I was going to be a mother. I was going to be responsible for another human life. *Oh, the travesty!* No, I wasn't going to think that way. I continued with the letter.

I'm a twenty-seven-year-old female and I like long walks on the beach.

What the hell? This wasn't a personal ad for Craigslist. I scratched that sentence out.

So, what's it like living in a ball of goo for nine months? Can you breath okay in there? I always wondered what it's like to go from breathing amniotic fluid to air. Remember to tell me about that, will ya?

I was asking my child scientific questions that it would have no recollection of me asking whatsoever. I needed to find a different topic.

I can't wait to find if you have a Ding Dong or a hot dog bun?

Fuck it! I threw the pad of paper and pen back on the coffee table and went to get ready to meet Ryan at the mall.

***

Ryan sat in the food court feverishly typing into his phone.

"Watcha doing there, tiny dancer?" I tried to peek over his shoulder.

"I signed up for a dating site. Someone replied to my profile so I was just writing back."

"And what is the name of the sperm donor?"

"Tate." Ryan gave me a shy smile as he put his phone back in his pocket.

"And what does Tate look like?" I tried reaching my hand into Ryan's pocket so I could see the mysterious profile.

"Moxie, that's not my phone!" he hollered, moving back to get my hand out of his pocket.

"Oops, sorry about that." I bent over and spoke directly to Ryan's crotch. "Sorry about that, little pecker. It's all good. I have a vagina, nothing you'd be interested in."

Ryan readjusted himself, grabbed my arm, and led me toward the store. "I'm going to make you wear extra belly pillows for that."

When we walked into A Pea in the Pod, I instantly felt bile rise into my throat. I stood still, looking around the store filled with all things maternity, from clothes and undergarments the size of a small county to things to attach to boobs that milked them like a cow. A tiny girl who was a little too perky and zealous bounced up to Ryan and me.

"Welcome to A Pea in the Pod," she squeaked.

"Umm, hi," I said as I looked around the store. "Do you know where your mommy is?"

She giggled and shook her head. "I work here."

"Did they lower the minimum age for working minors? I don't want to get caught in the child labor law dispute," I said, as I looked up at the ceiling to see if there were hidden cameras. "Do they pay you in money or fish and gruel?"

"I get that a lot, actually I'm twenty-two. My name is Tina. What can I help you find?" she asked, still smiling.

I looked at Ryan for help. I wasn't sure the little nugget in front of us was going to be able to help this pregnant and extremely hormonal woman pick out clothes. Frankly, I was little afraid having her pick out items because she was small enough to get lost in the racks of clothes.

"My friend Moxie is in need of some new clothes to fit her... evolving body." Ryan told our tiny Tina.

I punched him in the arm. "I'm pregnant, asshole, not a Neanderthal growing into a human."

Tina laughed. "Of course. Moxie, is this your first time

shopping for maternity clothes?"

"There was this time at Target that I found these amazing jeans. They were so comfortable. They were in the maternity section and had a stretchy band across the waist."

"That must have been embarrassing to return," Ryan said.

"Who said I returned them? I haven't found jeans that comfortable ever since."

"Come with me and we can pick out some items that look like your style. The goal is to be fashionable, yet comfortable." Tina took my hand.

"Let's start with the sweatpants section," I told her as she led me to the back of the store.

Forty minutes later I had a heaping pile of clothes to try on in the dressing room. Everything from casual, work, and dressy clothes. Tina informed me to get a variety of items that I would need for the near future. I could always come back as my pregnancy progressed. I took that as code for "I'll take some of your paycheck now and the rest in installments for the next several months."

"I am so excited." Ryan clapped his hands and bounced on the balls of his feet. He planted himself on the bench in the dressing room.

"What do you think you're doing? I'm going to try this stuff on."

"I know, go right ahead." He waved his hand at all the clothes I had hung up.

"But you're sitting in the dressing room, how am I going to change?"

"Moxie, it isn't like I haven't seen naked women before. Even though I'm gay, I do know what boobs and twats look like." He crossed his legs, making himself comfortable.

"Unless you want my super growing boobs to poke your eyes out, I strongly suggest you wait out there." I pointed to the chair outside the dressing room.

He got up, grumbling something about hormones and bitches, and sat outside the dressing room. I lifted my shirt over my head and unzipped my pants, letting them fall to the floor. I took a moment to look at my body in the dressing room mirror. There it was, my baby bump. I rubbed my hand over it, surprised how hard it felt. I hoped I wasn't growing a boulder. I picked up the first pair of pants, tilting my head to one side to study them. They weren't bad looking, and they had that same stretchy material as the jeans I got from Target. I stepped into them and slid them up my legs. I pulled the band over my stomach and looked into the mirror. Instant tears sprang to my eyes and a wail tore out of my mouth.

"Moxie? What's wrong? Let me in." Ryan pounded on the door in a panic.

I opened the door and stood there only in the pants and my bra.

"What is it? Are you in pain? Should I call Miles?"

"No." I sniffled.

"Then what is it?"

I put both of my hands on my stomach and looked down and back up at Ryan. "I'm in love with maternity pants."

Eighteen

Miles

"You look great!" I said as Moxie gave me a runway show for me in her new clothes.

I was happy she and Ryan had gone shopping for maternity clothes. For one, I knew Ryan would be able to take Moxie's wrath when something didn't fit or she felt like an inflated balloon. And two, I absolutely abhorred shopping. Sure, I shopped when I needed to, but if I had a choice to be in a pit full of snakes or walk around Macy's, I would take snakes any day. I knew nothing when it came to clothes, and I knew double nothing when it came to maternity clothes. All I understood was that pants were supposed to the stretchy. Actually, I wished I had some maternity jeans after s a Thanksgiving meal.

"I feel like a whale. But a really cute whale with trendy leggings and white button-down shirt and turquoise jewelry.

"I don't think my parents are going to be looking at your outfit."

Note: Wrong thing to say to someone when they're hormonal.

"What? I spent all fucking afternoon with Ryan trying on a bazillion outfits to impress your parents. I was even attacked by breast milk pads!"

I had to think if I really wanted to know what breast milk pads were, but I thought better of it since Moxie was already on edge. I had called my parents shortly after meeting Moxie's dad and Martha; it was time they also knew about the wedding and the baby. They knew that I had every intention of proposing to Moxie, but they were surprised when I told them about the pregnancy. Actually, my mom was surprised, I my dad's reaction was, "Danes have super sperm. Way to get one past the goalie, son."

My parents loved being grandparents. When we lived in Maine they would spoil Dillion endlessly. They also loved to hug, cuddle, and kiss him whenever he stayed at their house overnight. After the car accident they never left Dillion's side. They knew that while I was with Dillion, I was grieving the loss of my wife. I was lucky to have their support; I don't know if I would have made it without them. Dad was a lawyer and Mom was a teacher like Moxie. Both of them took time off their jobs to help me care for Dillion when he was released from the hospital.

"Sweetness, we need to go. The dinner reservation is at six and we need time to get there."

"Is that because it takes your pregnant fiancée forever to move from place to place? Maybe we should consider renting a crane."

I moved closer Moxie and cupped her cheeks. I looked into the deep blue eyes I loved so much and felt a rush of peace run through me. She made me so happy.

"I want you to listen very closely, Moxie Summers. I love you. I love the way your body is changing because inside of you is a life we created together. I know that this is all new to you and you have your insecurities about it. But never doubt that I think you're beautiful." I placed my hand on her stomach and swept her hair aside with my other hand and kissed her forehead.

"Thank you," she whispered, placing her hand on top of mine.

"We're leaving early because I know you're going to ask me to stop at least ten times to pee." I gave her a wry smile.

"If you just let me get a funnel and a soda can like I suggested, that wouldn't be an issue."

"How about strap a Porta-Potty to the hood of the car?" I laughed, knowing her intense hatred of Porta-Potties.

I shivered at the thought as I went toward Dillion's room to see if he was ready to go. I wanted tonight to be a family gathering. Even Kelly and her boyfriend, John, were meeting us at the restaurant. I got everyone into the car and was ready to go when Moxie said she needed to pee one more time before we left. When she came back to the car she was carrying a funnel with her from the kitchen. I shook my head and she just laughed, making a pissing sound with her mouth as if she were going to go in my car.

We pulled up to the restaurant and I had the valet park my car. I was feeling a little nervous about the initial meeting. Not because I didn't think my parents weren't going to like Moxie, just the opposite. Since Moxie had her own family issues, I worried she had aversions to all things parental. But I hoped by seeing how nurturing my own parents were, Moxie would realize there was such a thing and she would be just as nurturing to our baby.

We decided to meet at an upscale steak house. The break from McDonalds was very much welcome. Kelly and John were waiting in the entry way for us and Dillion bolted into Kelly's arms, giving her a big hug. Kelly had my mom's blond hair and cornflower blue eyes. She was considered model pretty, but the thought of her modeling anything less than a nun's habit sent me reeling. I was her older brother, and it was my job to protect her. To my relief she was a black belt in tae kwon do so I was pretty sure she would be able to take anyone down in the room. I liked John a lot. He was a bald guy with lots of tattoos. To the average person he looked pretty bad ass, but he couldn't be a nicer guy. Moxie liked to call him *Crouching Bad Ass, Hidden Pussy*.

"We're is my beautiful boy?" Mom shrieked as soon as she was in the restaurant.

"Right here, Mom." I stretched out my arms to give her a hug.

"Not you, idiot. My grandchild."

"I feel so loved," I mumbled.

"Grandma!" Dillion let go of Kelly and ran into Mom's arms.

Dad walked in after Mom. He was the kind of man who got along with everyone, no matter who they were or what they did. He managed to find a topic of conversation to suit every person. Mom was always adamant I got my good looks from him, which of course, meant he was a stud muffin. He had the same brown hair as mine, but his was graying on the sides. He said it was because my mother made him insane, but I've never seen two people who were more in love than them.

"Hello, son," he said, giving me a man hug and patting me on the back.

I pulled Moxie to my side and I felt her drag her heels.

"Dad, this is Moxie. Moxie, this is my dad, Kyle."

"So this in the famous Moxie," he said, taking Moxie's hand.

"I swear I didn't do it. I only tried pot once and had hallucinations of Tom Petty afterward," she said nervously.

Dad let out a big belly laugh and pulled Moxie in for a

hug. Moxie seemed a little taken aback by this and raised her eyebrows at me over my dad's shoulder. Then Mom came over to my side and looked at Moxie. She was silent for a moment and Moxie looked like she was going to be sick under her scrutiny.

"Do you know how much I've wanted redheaded grandchildren?" Mom's eyes lit up and a smile spread wide on her face. Moxie's shoulders dropped and she relaxed. My mom grabbed her for a hug and this time all Moxie could do was smile.

The host led us to our table and handed out menus. My heart beat faster when Moxie helped Dillion look over the menu before she even considered herself. It was just another reason why I thought Moxie was going to be a great mom. I just wished she saw the same thing.

"So, Moxie, did you have a hard time with morning sickness?" Mom asked.

"You could say that. I have plans to hold that over my child's head until the day I die. Every time they don't get their way I plan to tell them I don't care because I spent a month or two hugging the toilet on their behalf."

"I was so sick with Miles. In fact, I was sick pretty much my whole pregnancy."

"Oh God, does that mean this child is going to grow into another Miles? The world can barely handle one!" Kelly said with a dramatic flair.

"They can only handle one because I'm beyond perfect. If

the world had more than one it would explode because it can only handle so much greatness."

"I didn't know people with such power could fail Spanish in high school," Dad said, peeking over his menu at me.

"Listen, old man. That teacher hated me because I denied his advances."

"He did not come on to you," Kelly said, smacking her menu onto the table.

"Excuse me, his name was *Mr. Bendover* and he gave Hersey Kisses only to the boys in class."

The table erupted in laughs but was interrupted by an explosive sound followed by something that smelled like a dead body. Everyone looked around the table, and Moxie's face turned beet red.

"Ew, someone farted." Dillion covered this mouth and nose with his hand.

"I'm so sorry!" Moxie's hands flew to her face to cover up her embarrassment.

My jaw went slack as I stared at her, but was quickly replaced with laughter. Of all the time we have been together, I had never heard Moxie pass gas. I questioned whether or not her body was even human because nothing ever came out.

"Oh, honey. It's okay. It's the hormones and the pregnancy. It makes you very gassy," Mom tried to sooth her.

"Moxie, if it makes you feel better I can rip one out right

here. But I might end up killing the entire wait staff." Dad pretended to bear down and scrunched up his face.

"I'm going to die," Moxie said, still covering her face."

I reached over and put my arm around her shoulders and brought her close to me, kissing her head. I know she wanted to shrivel up and die, considering she wanted to make a good impression. But what a better way to make someone feel comfortable then knowing you can fart around them. We'll have to discuss if it's okay to fart around each other in the house because running into the other room was getting kind of tiresome.

We ordered our meals and talked about the baby and wedding plans. My parents asked Moxie a lot of questions without grilling her for information. As the evening progressed, Moxie was able to relax and even joke around with my parents. My Moxie, the one I knew and loved so much was back. And she was showing my parents all the reasons I fell for her in the first place.

Nineteen

Moxie

"What happens if it has a big mutant baby head? There is nothing worse than baby mutant heads. You know, where the baby's head is twice the size of its body? And everyone has to tell you how cute your baby is even though it looks like Frankenstein."

I looked out the window of Miles's car. We were on our way to the doctor's office for the ultrasound. To say I was nervous would be a slight understatement. Immensely terrified sounded better. Like having to take a shit in a gas station bathroom kind of terrified.

"What happens if it's got webbed feet? Then people will

follow him or her around quaking like a duck and call them Donald." I ran my hands down my face.

"Here's one," Miles added. "Maybe the baby is fine and normal and you have nothing to worry about."

I looked at him. "Have you met me? You should know that the words normal and fine are not part of my vocabulary. I am a Jew. It has been inbred into me over thousands of years to worry. If I didn't worry, I would be a disappointment to my entire religion."

"You can always go with the Catholic way of thinking."

"And what would that be?"

"Ignore everything and pretend it never happened."

I leaned my head back on the headrest and closed my eyes. What happens if it's born with multiple eyes? Maybe it wasn't Miles who impregnated me, but an alien. Oh my God! I'm having an alien baby. We pulled up to the doctor's office and Miles got out of the car. But I just sat there, feeling anxious. Miles came around to my side of the car and opened the door.

"Ready?" he asked as he extended his hand out for me to take.

"Do you think it's too late to ask for a return? Maybe I can get a nice coat or something."

"Last time I checked we were having a baby, not shopping at Nordstrom."

"But I saw these really cute pair of shoes—"

"Moxie, you have five seconds to get out of the car, or I will carry you and our baby over my shoulder into that office."

"Fine. But I could have gotten you a nice shirt and a pair of pants for the return."

Miles was sweet to help me out of the car, but since my body was changing, I was having to learn new ways of moving.

We walked into the waiting room and I approached the receptionist to sign in. "Hi. Moxie Summers. I'm here for my ultrasound," I said as a fidgeted with the sign-in sheet.

"Okay, great. I'll let them know you're here."

But I didn't move away from the desk. "I'm seeing the baby today." I informed the new victim of my nervous angst.

The receptionist looked around to see if I was speaking to someone behind her. When she realized the comment was directed at her she said, "Yes, I know. That's generally what happens during an ultrasound."

"Would you say that you see a lot of woman coming out of the ultrasound room crying or happy?"

The receptionist looked confused. "Umm, generally happy?"

"How many times have you heard people wailing from that room because something had gone wrong? Do they have a licensed psychologist on staff to council patients if the baby has extra appendages? Has anyone ran out of the office screaming?"

Miles put his large hands on my shoulders and a kissed the top of my head.

"You'll have to excuse my fiancée. She's a little nervous." Miles steered me away from the receptionist desk and to the seating area.

"I was simply asking the nice woman for some information," I said.

"You're going to get yourself locked up with the looney bin. Try to relax."

"You'll need to get me some of those elephant-sized tranquilizers for that to happen."

"Only if I get to shoot it into your sweet ass." He gave me that devious Miles smile.

"No sexy talk. Your smooth moves got us into this position."

"No, I believe it was me fucking you that got us into this position." He put his arm around me, pulled me into him, and snuggled and kissed my cheek. Before I could retort, Nurse Ratched called my name from the doorway.

Miles stood up and pulled me with him. I felt like a little kid being dragged by my parent out of a toy store.

Nurse Ratched, with her unwavering enthusiasm, led us to the ultrasound room. Without any acknowledgment she started shooting off the questions.

"Step on the scale."

"I don't weight myself," I answered.

She looked disapprovingly at me over the frames of her glasses just like the first time we met.

"What?" I asked defensively.

"You don't weigh yourself?"

"Why would I want to know how much my minion is taking up in my body?"

She rolled her eyes. "Step on the scale."

"No." I crossed my arms across my chest and started tapping a foot.

Next thing I knew Miles arms were around me, picking me up, and setting me down on the scale. I glared at him.

"I don't want to know." I squeezed my eyes shut and plugged my ears with my fingers.

After a moment the nurse tapped my shoulder and pointed for me to step off the scale. Relieved, I got off and started to walk toward the exam table. But Nurse Ratched rattled off my weight over my shoulder. I cringed and gave her a dirty look. She opened a drawer, took out a sheet of paper, and laid it on the table.

"The technician will come in shortly," she said and exited the room.

"Isn't she a delight," Miles deadpanned.

"Don't look directly in her eyes." I wagged my finger at him. "You might turn into stone."

"Let me help you change," Miles said.

"You just want an opportunity to take my clothes all the way off."

"I was just trying to be helpful."

I placed my hands on my hips and looked at him like a mother waiting for her child to cough up the truth.

"Fine, I wanted to cop a feel, even if you don't have to take off your shirt. I can't help it. Your boobs are massive and demanding to be touched."

"Last time I checked tits didn't talk." I tried my best to acted pissed, but couldn't help my smile.

"Sweetness, your tits call to me twenty-four seven."

I rolled my eyes and hopped up onto the table. There was a knock at the door and a woman looked in.

"Moxie?"

"Depends. Do I owe you money?"

She laughed and entered the room. "I'm Trisha, your ultrasound tech. Are you ready to see what's cooking in there?"

"You mean there are other things besides babies you could find in there? Do you ever get women claiming they've been probed by aliens and then find an alien baby growing in their uteruses?"

"No. Well, not today anyways," she said, winking. "Just lay back on the table. I'm going to squirt some jelly onto your belly and we can see what's going on.

I pulled my pants down and my shirt up to my bra so Trisha could squeezed the bottle of cold lubricant onto my stomach and put the ultrasound wand on top. Miles grabbed ahold of my hand. We both watched the screen, waiting for something that looked like a life form. Trisha moved the wand over my rounded stomach and something came into view on the screen. Miles and I both squinted. It looked like one of those ink Rorschach tests. Trisha kept moving the wand around to get a better angle.

"There we go," Trisha said in a singsong voice. "There is an arm and another arm." She stopped the wand and hit some keys on the ultrasound machine. "And there is the head and…" She paused with a look of confusion. She reached for my chart that was sitting on the table next to her and flipped through it.

"What? Why did you just pause? It's an alien, isn't it? It has the head of a cow! I knew I shouldn't have eaten so much meat." I said, starting to sweat.

Trisha placed the wand back on my stomach and moved it around until the form came back onto the screen. When it was visible, she pointed to it. "This is the baby's head." Then she moved the wand slightly. "And this is the other baby's head."

Silence draped the room. My eyes didn't leave the screen in what felt like minutes.

"My baby has two heads!" I screamed, tears welling up in my eyes.

"No! No, Moxie." Trisha turned to me. "Moxie, you're having twins."

I suddenly went deaf. Trisha's mouth kept moving and her face contorted with excitement, but no sounds came out. I thought I could make out Miles's voice, but all that kept ringing in my ears was the word *twins*. Twins. Two babies. Twice the poopy diapers. Two more therapy bills to pay.

"Moxie? Sweetness? Are you okay?

"I'm having a two-headed alien baby," I muttered, still dazed.

Miles chuckled and pulled me close to him. He kissed my cheek and said, "We never do things halfheartedly, do we?"

"Would you like to know the sex of the babies?" Trisha asked.

"No sex. Sex makes two-headed alien babies," I mumbled.

"Yes, we want to know," Miles answered for both of us.

"Okay. Baby A is a boy. And baby B is a girl."

"Holy fuck," was all I could add.

"Congratulations," Trisha said.

Finally, my eyes moved off the screen and I looked at Miles, who was glowing with an enormous smile. Then I looked back at Trisha.

"I think you might have your first patient running out of here screaming."

Twenty

Miles

Moxie and I walked into the hospital for our first birthing class. I remembered some of the classes I took with Sarah before Dillion was born, so to me this was a refresher course. We learned things like how to change a diaper, how to feed the baby, and how not to freak out when the baby sticks a cufflink your dad gave you up their nose. Moxie's belly was definitely growing as our twins lounged nicely in Casa de Moxie. The other day she came to me in a panic saying she thought her pancreas was ready to explode. She showed me where the pain was and I pressed on her stomach only to be kicked back from one of the kids. When I told her it was only the baby kicking, she yelled at her stomach to knock it off. Mommy still needed her pancreas.

We also started talking about baby names, which was an interesting conversation. I wanted to choose something different that would make them stand out like Moxie's name. She said she would take a baseball bat to anyone who made fun of our kids' names. Therefore the names Elsabub and Gasto were out. Moxie wanted to represent her mom's name because that was a Jewish tradition. You were supposed to name someone after the dead. When I asked her if we could name our son Miles Junior, she snapped at me, and said if I don't rub her swollen feet, she'd kill me. In the end she said we could use the name *Miles*.

"Do you know what floor we're supposed to be on?" Moxie asked.

I looked at the paperwork. "Sixteenth floor, room sixteen oh eight."

We got into the elevator with an older woman and her husband and pressed the button for the sixteenth floor. Moxie rested her hands onto of her growing belly. I thought that was one of the most adorable things. I placed my hands on her stomach and kissed her forehead.

"I love you," I said into her hair.

"Love you, too."

"It's so nice seeing young people in love," the little old lady said. "You must be due any minute."

I felt Moxie tense. She was feeling insecure with how big she was getting, and we still had a while to go until the babies came. I took the situation into my own hands before there was a little old lady bloody carcass on the floor.

"We still have a while to go. We're having twins."

"Oh gracious. You have two to push out!"

I covered Moxie's mouth with a kiss because I knew she was getting ready to tell this woman to shove her husband's cane up her ass. We got lucky and the elevator dinged for our floor. I took Moxie's hand and led her out of the elevator.

But before it closed, Moxie snuck the last words to the couple. "Old people die here every day. Are you next?"

I laughed a little, still dragging Moxie by the hand to find the correct room we were supposed to be. Once we found it, we opened the door. There were four other couples already sitting on the floor. It looked as if the women were in different stages of pregnancy. Moxie and I found a place next to a couple who looked pretty young. I helped Moxie lower herself down on the floor before I sat down next to her.

The guy sitting next to me gave me a manly head tip. "Hey, man. I'm Robby and his is my girl, Suzy"

"Hey, I'm Miles and this is my fiancée, Moxie." Moxie and Suzy gave each other a slight wave.

"Is this your first kid?" Robby asked.

"We have another son who's seven." When I said this, Moxie looked at me with mixed emotions. She needed to come to terms that Dillion was her son as much as he was mine. I hadn't told her yet, but Dillion asked me the other day if he could start calling Moxie *mom*. I told him that it was something he was going to have to talk to her about. I knew Moxie loved Dillion with all of her heart. But there was a piece of me that didn't want to tarnish Dillion's memories of Sarah.

"How about you? Do you have any other kids?" I asked Robby in return.

"I have five other kids. But this is my first one with Suzy."

My eyes widened. Robby looked like a kid himself. I couldn't help but ask. "How old are you guys?"

"I'm twenty-one and Suzy is nineteen. We met at Chick-fil-A when I was working the night shift. I saw her ass and knew she was the one for me."

"Oh, Robby. Stop talking sweet." Suzy squeezed Robby's arm and then she turned to me. "His other baby mamas are such whores who only want Robby for his money."

I was in too much shock to respond.

But Moxie wasn't. "I can only imagine. Chick-fil-A must bring in the big bucks."

A plump woman with short brown hair and glasses came into the room just before I was about to ask Robby if he knew what condoms were.

"Hi, everyone! My name is Heather. We are going to get started for the evening. We have many things planned for you including breathing techniques, how to handle a baby, a birthing video, and a lactation consult to talk about breastfeeding. So let's begin!"

We learned some different breathing techniques to use during labor. Moxie lay between my legs and I rubbed her shoulders, coaching her along the way. I couldn't help but nuzzle my nose into her hair and breathe in that amazing shampoo she used.

"Are you getting hard?" she whispered, turning her head to look at me.

"I can't help it, you're sitting between my legs, I'm rubbing your shoulders, and smelling your hair."

"You get hard smelling my hair? Do you have some hair fetish now?"

"I like the way your shampoo smells. Sometimes I use it as lube and jerk off in the shower."

"What!" Moxie screamed, making everyone in the room look at her.

"Sorry, everyone. She thought I said two breaths out instead of one. She suffers from OCD," I said, trying to make an excuse for Moxie's outburst.

"I was wondering why my shampoo was disappearing. I thought it was pregnancy brain, and I was using more than I thought. I'm never going to look at Herbal Essences the same way," she whispered.

After breathing exercises, we moved to another exercise

using fake babies. I let Moxie take the lead on this one since I'd had plenty of practice in the past with Dillion. I didn't think Moxie had changed a diaper in her entire life. Granted, when she taught kindergarten last year, she claimed that half of her kids still needed to be in diapers because they seemed to miss the toilet.

"Everyone, in front of you is your baby already wearing their diaper."

Moxie raised her hand.

"Yes, dear?" Heather asked.

"What kind of diapers are we talking about? Huggies? Luvs? Costco? Do we use cloth diapers? I'm not really keen on throwing my kids crap in the toilet every time they poop. And since we're on the subject, let's talk diaper wipes. Are you thinking sensitive or non-sensitive? Will the scented kind irritate their ass? I also read that different diapers are better for boys than girls. We're having twins. Are you telling me we have to buy two different brands?"

Heather's eye started to twitch at all of Moxie's questions. I quietly snickered to myself.

"I would say that it's all trial and error. What might work for one baby might not work for another. You might have a baby with sensitive skin or a child that wets the diaper more in front than back," Heather said.

"My kids would just probably wet the whole damn diaper. Maybe I should put two diapers on them," Moxie said, rubbing her chin with her fingers.

Heather shook her head and continued with her demonstration. "Now, each of you open your baby's diaper by tearing the tabs on the sides."

Moxie gingerly opened the diaper and pulled it away from the doll.

"Oh my God!" she yelled as she jumped back from the doll. "My doll shit in its diaper!"

I leaned over her shoulder to see what she was looking at and laughed. In the diaper was a smashed Snickers bar to simulate real poop.

"Why? Why would you subject a Snickers bar to such a horrible death? What did it ever do to you?"

"Moxie, we put the Snickers bar in for several reasons," Heather tried to explain. "First we want to show the proper way of cleaning a baby's bum. Secondly, we want to discuss what abnormalities you might find in your child's feces and what you should do."

Moxie immediately raised her hand again.

"Yes, Moxie," Heather said with a groan.

"Why would my baby have peanuts in their poop?"

"Because maybe it accidently found a bag and swallowed some," Heather said, grabbing the diaper and throwing it in the trash can.

As the class went on, Heather showed us how to swaddle the baby in a blanket. Moxie got so frustrated because she couldn't get the technique down, so she stomped out of the class, mumbling something about it being bullshit and how it's all a conspiracy.

After coaxing her back, the thing that further tipped the scales was the birthing video. It was like sitting with someone during a horror movie. Moxie covered her eyes for most of the video, peeking through her fingers on occasion and burying her head into my shoulder.

Finally the lactation consultant came in to do her presentation on breastfeeding. The way that I look at, I felt it was a woman's choice if she decided to breastfeed. It wasn't my breasts that got sucked on hours on end throughout the day. Although, any extra chance I got to see a woman's breast was always an extra bonus. Sarah breastfed Dillion until he turned one, but that was her choice. She felt it was the best option for him and that it was a way for them to bond. Moxie and I hadn't had the conversation about breastfeeding, so I was curious what she thought.

"Hello, everyone. My name is Angela and I am the lactation consultation for the hospital. I am the one that comes into your room after you have your baby to help you get started on your journey to breastfeeding."

Moxie tensed up. This wasn't a good sign as her body usually tensed before an emotionally explosion. I rubbed her back in hopes of calming her down. Angela brought out a contraption from her tote that looked like a fake pair of breast connected to a harness. She proceeded to put the harness over her own chest to make it look like she was naked from the waist up. The sight was disturbing. It reminded me of a freak show at a circus. The worse part came next as she brought out a baby doll that had a puckered mouth.

"It's important to get to know the signs when your baby is ready to eat. When they are first born, they make a motion with their mouth as if they were sucking. This is called rooting, and it's a sign that they're searching for your nipple."

Next to me Robby imitated a rooting face to Suzy.

"I'm in search of your nipple, babe. Why don't you whip it out for me."

"Ahem." Angela gave Robby a scolding look and Robby bowed his head down in shame.

Angela continued her instruction, discussing latching , the comfort zone for nipple placement, and what to do if you get sores on the breast from nursing. Toward the end I was feeling a little nauseated when she told us a story about a woman suffering from mastitis but still very determined to breastfeed her child. Moxie still looked wound up.

When she raised her hand, I had to admit, I was feeling a little nervous not knowing what she was going to ask.

"Yes, Moxie?"

"I don't plan on breastfeeding. I want to leave the privilege of sucking my nipples to my fiancé. In fact, it's a huge turn on for me when he does it and I would like to keep it that way. Plus, I have big knockers to begin with, and I don't want these puppies sinking to the floor because they were used as a feeding trough for my kids."

Oh shit. Angela looked at Moxie like someone just ran

over her dog.

"Moxie, breast is best when it comes to the nourishment of your child. There is an abundant amount of research that proves that breast milk is the best way to protect your child from illness and for healthy brain development," Angela said, trying to sound professional. Honestly, she looked like she was about to lose her shit.

"So you're telling me I'm going to have sick, stupid children because I won't share my boobs with them?"

"Sweetness, I think she's just trying to do her job," I said, taking her hand and tenderly squeezing it.

"Look, buddy." Moxie pointed at my chest with her free hand. "I'm trying to protect your playthings and Tit Hitler here is trying to tell me we're are going to have dysfunctional children because I won't give it up for them. It's our job as parents to make them dysfunctional, not my rack!"

"You tell 'em, sista," Robby added.

I couldn't contain my laughter because Moxie was being, well, Moxie. My little spitfire was just speaking her truth. I took hold of her elbow and helped her out of the chair.

"I think it's time to excuse ourselves. Thank you for the information and good luck to everyone here," I said, leading Moxie to the door. But before we could make it all the way out, Moxie had to get the last word in to Angela.

"I hope your fake boobs sag to the ground and your plastic baby has to sit on the floor to eat!"

The Pregnancy Guide

Months 7 and 8

Women

Congratulations, you've made it to the last trimester of your pregnancy. During this time a lot of women start to nest, making sure the nursery is ready and all the clothes are bought. You will also feel your little boy or girl kick more. Maybe they're going to be little soccer players! You might feel a little warm as your hormones continue to change. Remember that fatigue you felt during that start of your pregnancy? It will become more prominent, so don't feel bad taking naps so your body can recharge. You also may feel the need to urinate more, so make sure you always know where a bathroom is in case you have to relive yourself.

Men

This is it! This is the time you're going to be able to have sex with your partner again. That's if she can stay awake long enough to have sex. Don't give up hope, you might be able to sneak something between bathroom breaks. Also invest in a hat, gloves, and a thermal jacket. Your partner will want the air conditioner on at full blast, even if it's the dead of winter. At this point you'll be pretty sure your partner is having an alien. Her stomach will move and roll on its own accord. Just remember, they come in peace.

Twenty-one

Moxie

I woke up and reevaluated my surroundings. I was in a bed under a down comforter that was making me sweat, but a pair of cold feet rubbed up my leg. Cold feet next to mine. I knew those cold feet and they didn't belong to Miles.

"How they hell does Raj put up with those ice cubes you call feet?" I asked Renee in my sleepy haze.

She was already sitting up in bed, drinking a cup of coffee.

She smiled down at me like she'd just won the lottery.

"It's your wedding day!"

Renee insisted staying with me last night instead of Miles, reminding us that the groom wasn't allowed to see the bride before the wedding. I then reminded Renee that I was very pregnant and the whole virtuous bride idea flew out the window the second the stick turned pink.

I lay in bed, thinking about Miles and how today we would officially be married. It was then that Mortimer and Can-d-Cane decided to kick me under my ribs. Miles and I still hadn't settled on names, so I came up with something different every day.

"Jesus Christ, I'm getting up, you two," I said to my stomach.

"Aww. Are they kicking?" Renee asked in a goochie, goochie, goo voice.

I scowled. "Talk to me in that voice again and I will demonstrate how hard they're kicking me in your ass."

"Come on, we need to start getting ready. The makeup artist and hair person will be here in twenty minutes. I got you some decaf and pastries we can munch on while we get ready."

"I was going to profess my undying love to you, but then you said it was decaf coffee." I groaned.

"No caffeine for you until those babies are out."

In a huff, I got out of bed and put the robe on, tying it

around my very swollen belly. I waddled over to the table in the room and grabbed a Danish out of the pastry basket. "So where are the dresses?" I asked, with a mouth full of Danish.

"Martha had them steamed and pressed. She said they would send them up when they were done. Are you feeling excited? Nervous? Anxious? All of the above?"

"I feel weird. Don't get me wrong, I don't have any doubts about marrying Miles, but this isn't how I pictured things would go. I had a different vision in my head about my wedding. But with Dad being terminally ill, I wanted to give him the wedding he wanted to give his daughter before he died." My heart sunk as the words came from my mouth.

Renee took in a deep breath. "Moxie, I understand you wanted to do this for your dad. But why didn't you ever talk to him about this and tell him what you really wanted? It is *your* wedding after all."

"Martha said he didn't want me to know about the cancer, that it would crush him. He didn't want me to worry about him and put stress on me and the babies. I mean it's just one day out of our lives. The important thing is that I'm with Miles, Dillion, and the babies. If it makes him happy that his daughter has a fairy-tale wedding, I can do that."

Renee gave me a half smile, knowing perfectly well this wasn't my dream, but my dad's. She put one hand on my shoulder. "You're a good woman, Moxie Summers. And you're right. It isn't about flowers or the cake, but spending your life with the person you love."

"What the fuck do you mean it's not about the cake? That

cake dictates how my life with Miles will be. It must be chocolate or all hell will break loose and we will be divorced within a month," I said, moving to get another Danish.

We both laughed when there was a knock at the door. Renee opened the door to a hotel employee holding two very large garment bags.

"I was asked to bring these up for Miss Summers," the employee said, straining to keep the garment bags from falling off his fingers."

"I'll take those, thanks." Renee took the bags and closed the door with her foot.

"Holy crap, these are heavy for two tea length dresses." She patted the bag with her free hand. "And what the hell did they put in here? Tissue paper?"

I walked over to the bags. "Let's hang them in the closet and take a look. We opened the first bag and stumbled back in complete shock when we saw a plum colored floor length satin dress and matching shawl.

"What the fuck is this?" I quickly moved the dress away and pulled the zipper on the second garment bag. "Oh my fucking Lord, "I said in a whisper.

Renee moved to my side and saw the horror. It was the white marshmallow dress that I tried on at the boutique. The tulle came pouring out of the bag onto the floor. Rhinestones and beadwork flickered with the light coming in from the window. To top it off, a long veil with a large crown hung from the hanger. About two minutes passed before either of us could say anything. We just stood there, looking at the dress in utter horror.

"There has to be a mix up," Renee finally said.

"Get. My. Phone," I replied through gritted teeth.

Renee rushed over to my bag and dug my phone out for me. I found the number I needed. It only took one ring before she answered.

"Good morning, beautiful bride. Are you ready to wed your prince charming?"

"Martha, there is a problem with the dress." I tried to remaining as composed as possible.

"Oh God! Did they press the tulle down to much? I told them it was supposed to be flowing, like you'd be on a cloud."

"This isn't the dressed I picked out." I clutched the fabric of the dress, still trying to keep calm.

"I know, dear, but I showed your father all the pictures we took of you in the dresses and he just instantly fell in love with this one. He even had tears in his eyes." Martha's voice cracked,

"Martha, I'm going to look like the fucking Stay Puft Marshmallow Man."

"Moxie, watch your language. The dress is stunning on you and it's what your father dreamed of you in. Put aside your selfishness for one second and remember he is paying for this wedding. He wants to see his daughter walk down the aisle in a beautiful dress."

Before I could string together a long sentence of swear words, I ended the call. I walked toward the bed and sat, putting my hands on my belly.

"Kids, Mommy might be in jail for murder in the first degree when you are born. Don't worry. I'll have Daddy bring you to visit."

Renee sat on the bed beside me. "Look at it his way, when Miles says he wants to eat you, he'll be talking about the dress instead of your cooch because you'll look like whipped cream."

"I will never eat whipped cream again," I said, shaking my head. "Okay, I won't eat whipped cream for several months. Forever seems a bit overzealous."

About two hours later, my makeup was caked on. I say caked on because it was done so thick you could cut it with a knife. The hairstylist took my hair and turned it into someone from *Toddlers and Tiaras* would appreciate. I had to sit still while she made tight ringlets with a curling iron. When I told her I had to get up and pee, she said I would interrupt her creative space if I moved. I said her creative space was going to drown in urine if I didn't hit the bathroom immediately. Finally, she piled the curls on top of my head and incased them into the crown Martha had picked out.

The whole time I kept thinking of my dad and how proud and amazed he would be when he saw me. I was doing this ridiculousness for him. Even though my relationship was halfhearted or if there was a heart at all with Martha, I still loved my dad.

"Ready to put on the Cool Whip dress?" Renee pressed her lips together to repress her laughter.

I sneered at her like she just took my favorite dessert away. "I'll remember this one day when you get married and someone accidentally pisses all over your dress. I'm having children, remember? They will be my spawns and do what their master tells them. If I say whip it out and tinkle on Aunt Renee's dress, they will obey."

Renee bit her lip, trying to contain her laughter. Gathering the material, Renee slipped the dress over my head, allowing the tulle to fall to the floor. I put my arms through the sleeves, which were bedazzled with rhinestones and beads. Finally, Renee pulled the shoes out of their box and started laughing.

"Now what?" I sighed.

She turned to show me the shoes—white, five-inch stilettos.

"She got me *fuck me heels*?"

"Maybe she thought you could go stripping after the wedding?"

I grabbed the shoes from Renee, sat on the bed, and tried them on."

"There's no way I'm getting them on. I can't see what the hell I'm doing between my stomach and the pool of white."

Renee moved to the bed and took the shoe from my

hand. "Let me help my preggo petunia."

I took the other shoe and swatted her arm. Renee bent in front of me and tried putting the shoe on my foot.

"Umm, Moxie? The shoe won't fit. Your feet are too swollen."

"What? Great, now I'll have to go barefoot. I get to be the hippy pregnant bride who isn't even getting married on the beach."

"Yes, but you're the most beautiful hippy pregnant bride I know, and I'm so proud of you." Renee bent down and gave me a kiss on my forehead.

With Renee's help I launched myself from the bed to stand up. "Are you ready to go and become Mrs. Miles Dane?"

"Oh, didn't I tell you? Miles is taking my last name."

"Really?" Her eyes widened and eyebrows lifted.

"No, you dumb ass. I'm ready to ditch this name." I winked at her and linked my arm into hers.

We took the elevator down and walked toward the ballroom. Julie, the crazy coordinator, was there waiting for us.

"Moxie, you look like a snow princess!" she bellowed

"More like a snow yeti," I said under my breath.

"Everything is almost set and all of the guests have arrived. I think you will be simply overwhelmed with how stunning it all is." Julie clapped her hands together.

"Is Miles and Dillion down yet?" I asked.

"Yes and they are anxiously waiting your arrival. I will escort you two to the ballroom. Your dad is waiting to walk his beautiful bride down the aisle."

Renee gave me a sad smile. Dad was waiting to walk me down the aisle. A dream that he had been holding on for so long. And now, when he's gone, I will have that memory to keep with me. Julie walked us the rest of the way to my dad who was pacing. He tugged his collar, looking very uncomfortable in his tux. Then he saw me and smiled. I strode up to him, trying to burn this memory into my brain.

"Hi, Dad," I said, choking up.

"Moxie, there are no words," he said, engulfing me into his arms.

I wondered if he was left speechless because this is how he imagined me. A giant, barefoot, pregnant cream puff.

Julie handed Renee and I our bouquets and I looked at her in confusion. "Julie, these aren't roses. They're lilies. I hate lilies."

She seemed to be surprised by this statement. "Your mother said that these lilies fitted the theme more than the roses.

"She's not my mother," I said, quickly remembering Dad was there. My own words of *stop being selfish* rang in my ears. "They're fine." I faked a smile to make my dad happy.

"Okay then, places!" Julie howled.

Renee stood in front of me and Dad, leading the procession. Julie mumbled something into her earpiece and I suddenly heard the music start to play.

"Is that an organ playing?"

Julie ran up to me and quietly whispered, "Your mom thought it sounded more regal."

Turning my head so Dad wouldn't see my clenched my teeth, I whispered back to Julie. "She's not my fucking mother." But before she got the chance to respond the doors flew open.

I heard Renee's sharp intake of breath and moved around her to see what was going on. I stood there, frozen at the display in front of me. Lilies covered the entire aisle. The smell was so pungent it reminded me of a funeral parlor trying to cover up the smell of the dead. There was a hot pink runner going down the aisle that said *Moxie and Miles*. There must of been three hundred people in the room sitting on chairs that had matching hot pink bows on the backs. To my right in the distance, the wedding cake stood on a table. It had multiple tiers held together by columns and what looked like a water fountain springing from the top.

In the chaos I looked for Miles. He stood at the end of the aisle. As always he was breathtakingly beautiful, but I couldn't focus on him because of the canopy of lilies above him.

"Julie. Where is the chuppah made from my mom's old wedding dress? You know, the canopy we Jewish people get married under?"

"Umm, your mom said that the lilies would be a better option. That you wouldn't want a rag above you when you got married."

Suddenly the colors in the room changed and all I saw was red. The last straw holding me together snapped and that's when all hell broke loose.

Twenty-two

Moxie

"She's not my fucking mother!" I screamed. Three hundred heads turned toward me screaming at the wedding coordinator in the doorway of the ballroom.

"Houston, we have a problem," Julie said into her wireless headset.

People murmured as the organ music stopped. Thank

God for small favors. The smell of the lilies made my stomach turn.

Martha, who was dressed in white, stood from her chair and raised her hands in the air and addressed the guests. "I'm so sorry, everyone. I'll see what is going on. You know, hormonal bride and everything."

She walked up the aisle with Miles and Ryan following quickly behind her.

"What's wrong?" Miles grabbed me by the arms to make sure I was okay.

"What's wrong? What's wrong? This is wrong!" I waved around the room.

"Moxie Summers, calm down. Everyone is looking," Martha hissed.

"Of course, they're looking. They want to see the giant yeti coming down the aisle to swallow them whole."

"Moxie, honey, take it easy." Renee placed her hand on my shoulder, trying to calm me.

"No, I won't fucking take it easy." I shrugged Renee off.

"Moxie, why are you acting like a child?" Martha said in a low tone so the wedding guests wouldn't overhear.

Oh God, this woman didn't have a clue. Didn't she understand not to put her hand in the cage of an angry animal? On second thought, I hoped she stuck her hand in so it would get ripped off.

"Sweetness, what is it?" Miles said.

"This wedding... it's absurd. Have you seen me? I look like I was just squeezed out of the middle of an éclair!"

I waved toward the aisle. "It's hot pink. Hot fucking pink. I swear that color should have stayed in the eighties where it belongs. And an organ? This isn't a goddamned church."

I froze mid-tantrum, remembering my dad was standing next to me. Tears fell down my cheeks, and I grabbed Miles's hand trying to gain his strength.

"I'm sorry, Dad. I know this is what you dreamed for me, but I can't let this happen. Nothing in this reflects the love that Miles and I share, in the family we have created. Yes, I understand it's just a certificate saying that we're married, but it should be a day about us and not what others wanted for us."

Miles pulled me in and kissed my forehead. I knew he was beaming with pride that I'd finally spoken up even though there was a possibly of crushing Dad's dream.

"Moxie," Dad said, holding my arm, "What are you talking about?"

I looked up at him through tears. "I know, Dad," I said while I took the handkerchief out of the bouquet to wipe my makeup-stained cheeks.

"Moxie..." Martha hissed in warning.

Dad ignored his wife and continued. "Moxie, what do you know?"

"I know about the cancer, Dad. That this is what you wanted for a dying wish, to have a big wedding for me."

Uncomfortable silence swarmed in the air.

"I have cancer?" Dad asked in surprise.

Miles, Renee, Ryan, and I all looked at my dad like he lost his mind. This wasn't good if he was struggling with denial.

"Dad, you don't have to act like we're not supposed to know. Martha told us a while ago. She said that one of your dying wishes was to have this extravagant wedding for me."

All eyes turned to Martha, who was fiddling with a tissue in her hand. Sweat formed on her brow and she shifted nervously. I looked back to my dad.

"Sooo, you don't have cancer and you're not dying?

"Last time I went to the doctor he said my cholesterol was a little elevated and gave me some pills for my ulcer, but other than that I got a clean bill of health."

"But, what about this extravagant wedding that you wanted me to have?" My pulse picked up as everything clicked in my head.

"I didn't want a crazy wedding, Martha said this was your dream and being my only child, I wanted to make it special for you. If it were up to me, I would've given you cash and said go to Vegas."

My blood boiled. I was like a raging bull that had been stuck to many times in a bull fight. Martha had lied this entire time.

"It. Was. You." I put emphases on every word. I stalked slowly toward Martha.

"Things are about to get very, very ugly," I heard Ryan say to Miles.

"You fucking, sick, deranged woman. You set this whole thing up so it would go the way you wanted."

"Moxie, you are my only daughter and I wanted what was best for you. This a dream wedding, and I am is that you are acting so damned selfishly."

"You said my dad was dying!" My nose was flaring and my skin was flushed. I balled my hand into a fist and it took everything in me to not cock it back and punch her. Martha's lips were pursed together and her whole body stiffened.

"You wouldn't have listened otherwise. If it were up to you and this Gentile, you would have had a backyard picnic complete with a stuffed pig."

"How dare you think that's what we wanted. Or were you too busy planning all the ways you could make my life a living hell?"

I walked toward Martha as she backed into the ballroom. Heads were turning left and right, watching the battle.

"What insane asylum did they release you from before you met my father? Maybe we should have checked *America's Most Wanted* to see if you were on their list. Or better yet, check the zoo to see if one of their bitches escaped."

"Moxie, I will not let you speak to me like that. I have raised you as my own and demand respect."

This woman had lost her marbles, if she had any to begin with. Even though I still had a lot of pent up frustrations toward Martha I was willing to work on them for the sake of Dad. But I should have known and listened to my gut about her. I was beyond furious, but at the same time I was upset with myself for letting my guard down for even one second.

"Oh, you demand? Well, let me tell you what I demand. I want back all those fucking years you treated me like I was worthless because of my weight and that no one would love me because I was fat. I demand to get back all the opportunities to go to school dances because I was too self-conscious about going, afraid that no one would dance with the fat girl.

"Moxie, if you just eat this instead of that. Moxie, if you just wore your hair like this. Moxie, it would just put on a little makeup boys would notice you," I said, imitating Martha's nasally voice

Years of hateful words bubbled to the surface. The issue was plain and simple. I was never good enough. I was never the perfect daughter who would obey Martha's commands. I saw the people in the audience over Martha's shoulder. Most of them were standing and watching us like a movie, except we weren't actors. This was real life—my life.

"Moxie." I faintly heard Miles say my name. It was too late, I was mentally too far gone with too much pent up anger after so many years.

"Then you had the actual balls to disgrace my mother by saying her wedding dress was a rag? You're the fucking rag, Martha. You came in all those years ago and preyed on a grieving widower still mourning his dead wife. I didn't question it when I was younger, thinking that my dad was just lonely. But I never understood why he would be with such a lying, manipulative cunt like you."

After busting out the C word, a unified gasp came from the crowd. There weren't enough words to throw at this woman I loathed so much. It was at that moment I made the conscious decision that Martha would no longer be part of my life. I couldn't control what choices my father made, but there was no way this poisonous woman would be any part of my children's lives.

All of those scared feelings I had about becoming a mother centered around this woman. I was scared I would become her and treat my children as poorly as she did me. And now, when I felt my children move inside of me, I knew that there was no way I would let the poison from this woman reach any part of them.

"Moxie, since the day I met you, you have always been a rude, snotty, little brat who was ungrateful for everything anyone did for her. God would not bless me with my own children, so I did the best I could with what I had. I tried my best to push you in the right direction, but you've always been too stubborn to do anything except go your own way. I just hope that your children will be able to forgive you when they realize how selfish you are."

You know in the movies when everything around the lead character froze except them? Like in *The Matrix* when Keanu

Reeves jumped up in the air about to bring the shit down on Agent Smith? What happened next went a little something like that.

I pushed Martha with everything I had, and she fell back on the cake table. The cake came crashing down on her, making a mess all over the place. The cake had split into pieces all over the floor. The crowd erupted into gasps and cries. I tried bending down, but my swollen belly wouldn't let me, so I squatted and let one of my arms catch me as my ass made a loud thud onto the mess. I somehow spun around on my ass, using the frosting on the floor to my advantage and got onto my hands and knees like they showed Miles and I in our birthing class. I crawled over to Martha on the floor. I took pieces of crumbled cake and smashed it into Martha's face.

"Eat it!" I yelled. "Taste the fat!"

I took a big hunk of whipped icing and stuffed it into my mouth. With a full mouth, I screamed. A battle cry signaling my army to come join my cause. Arms surrounded me and pulled me to a standing position.

"Sweetness, calm down. It's okay." Miles rubbed my back in small circular motions.

"She didn't eat enough cake. She's still a skinny ass whore," I yelled, struggling to get out of Miles's embrace.

I suddenly stopped moving.

"Moxie, what's wrong?" he said as his eyebrows knitted together.

I slowing turned to face him. "Miles, either I just pissed

all over myself or my water just broke."

Twenty-three

Miles

I stood next to Moxie and looked at her dress, or what was supposed to be a dress; she was covered in cake. She stood in puddle of water, which I knew had nothing to do with the champagne on the cake table. Her water had broken during the argument. Apparently, my son and daughter wanted in on the fight with Martha.

"Are you okay?" I moved her out of the slippery icing on

the floor.

"My water broke, but it's too early for them to come. Hurry, mop it off the floor and stick the water back inside me!"

"Unfortunately, it doesn't work that way. We need to get over to the hospital. We can call Dr. Ford on the way," I said as I moved us through the throng wedding guests.

"Do you think preschool let out already? I mean, they shouldn't have had snack time. I don't want the doctor's blood sugar to drop when he's supposed to be watching my delivery hole." Dr. Ford wasn't as young looking as Moxie thought. At least, I didn't think so.

"I don't think anyone will miss your delivery hole."

"Are you saying I'm fat? You don't call a pregnant women fat! I'm in a marshmallow dress and you're calling me fat!" she yelled and flayed her hands around.

"That's not what I meant," I said as I took her in my arms and kissed her forehead.

Renee and Ryan ran up to get a better look at what was going on. A few people had gathered around Martha to help her up, but Moxie's dad was not one of them. In fact, Steven was nowhere to be seen.

"Ryan, go outside and have the valet pull the car around," I said.

He nodded and sprinted for the door of the ballroom.

"Your parents and Kelly are going to take Dillion with them," Renee said. "I'm not completely sure if they are aware your water broke, but they figured after that display with Martha you might have needed some time to yourself."

"Great. So now I'm fat and psychotic?" Moxie struggled to get out of my arms, but I held onto her. I didn't want her to hurt herself by trying to pull any of her Fish Ninja moves.

"Who said that?" Renee asked as she fisted her hands, ready to join Moxie's fight.

"No one," I said. "She is being a little irrational because of the excitement and her water breaking."

"I'm coming with you to the hospital," Renee added. "I have a feeling this is going to require some extra people. Especially if you value keeping your balls intact."

"Yes, I do value my balls, thank you." I guided Moxie to the main entrance.

"I'm fat, psychotic, and you have huge, low, hanging balls!" Moxie screamed.

The remaining guests gawked at me. I could feel my face flush and I gave a small smile. I said, "They're low hangers but very symmetrical."

I heard some people laugh, but the murmuring of the crowd drowned it out. All I cared about was getting Moxie to the hospital. She started to stumble and I looked down at her feet. She wore a pair of massive high heels and teetered with every step we took. I let go of her arms and bend down to take them off.

"Fantastic," she said. "Now I'm pregnant and barefoot. This is how you wanted me all along. Should I go find a kitchen to stand in so I can be your perfect little wife? Oh wait, I'm not your wife. Why? Because my evil stepbitch decided to create the wedding from hell and ruined everything. I'm going to have to live on welfare and food stamps."

I gave a puzzled look to Renee who had taken Moxie's other arm. Moxie was becoming delusional which made me more nervous. I had to remember she just in shock.

"Moxie, we have to go to the hospital now," I said in a calm voice. I had hoped that if I stayed calm, she would in turn calm down. Moxie grabbed her round belly with both hands and sweat beaded on her forehead.

"I'm not fucking going anywhere with someone who thinks I'm fat. Look at that woman over there." She pointed to a cake-covered Martha, surrounded people that might have actually given a rat's ass about her. "That bitch thought I was fat my whole damn life. I'm in a dress that looks like a jar of mayonnaise took a shit all over me!"

I gotten the impression Moxie wasn't going to move willingly, so I had no choice but to carry her out of here. I swept her into my arms.

"Put me down!" Moxie swatted my arms. "I am not *Free Willy*. You don't have to rescue me out of the waters of despair."

We arrived in the lobby and Ryan held the hotel door open. He gave me a look that said, "*What the hell? You're going to break your back carrying her.*" I shook my head, hoping he would get the message. Moxie would jump out of my arms and go all kung fu on his ass.

The valet had the passenger door of the SUV open, and I put Moxie down on her feet. I helped her in the vehicle as she started say something about how she was pissed that an innocent cake had to sacrifice itself for the cause. Renee got into the back seat of the car, and I ran to the other side to get into the driver's side. Renee rubbed Moxie's shoulders to comfort her, but Moxie just sat in the seat with her eyes closed and mouth rambling.

"Moxie, we're on our way to the hospital. I'm calling Dr. Ford so he can meet us there."

"My babies are going to come out looking like Oompa Loompas and be held captive in a chocolate factory. Then they will have to clean the tunnel of death."

"What's the tunnel of death?" Renee asked.

"You know, when Wonka takes everyone on the boat ride and it shows them cutting off the head of a chicken. My kids are going to have to clean up chicken goo."

Moxie then let out a small cry and put her hands back around her belly.

"I'm sorry, my little Oompas. I will talk to Wonka on your behalf."

"She's really losing it," Renee said.

I dialed Dr. Ford. He picked up after a few rings and his voice came over the Bluetooth of the car.

"Dr. Ford speaking."

"Dr. Ford, it's Miles Dane. Moxie's water just broke and we are on the way to the hospital."

"Isn't it nap time at the preschool? Dr. Ford, make sure you come with a clean diaper. Are you going to ride you tricycle there?"

There was a pause over the phone. I'm sure the doctor was confused as to what was happening.

"Dr. Ford, Moxie just experienced a traumatic episode and her water broke. She's not herself."

"Did she have an accident of some sort? Is she bleeding?"

"Umm, no," I said. "But she did just release eighteen years of repressed anger all at once."

"Check into the hospital and I will meet you there. Even though her water broke, it doesn't mean that she is going to delivery these babies any moment. We'll check to see if she is dilated. Is she experiencing any labor pains?"

"Not that I'm aware off. She's been having Braxton Hicks, but they've been resolving."

I knew this could be a long process from having gone through it before with Sarah and Dillion. Sarah was in labor with Dillion for twenty-three hours, but I wasn't about to tell Moxie that piece of information. She might hold a scalpel to a doctor's throat and demand they cut the babies out ASAP. I tried to relax the best I could, but I was worried Moxie was going to have a mental breakdown. All these months Martha had lied to us, telling us Moxie's dad was dying. Only because she wanted to have the wedding of *her* dreams. It was almost too much to believe. Steve must be a wreck. After getting Moxie settled, I'd call Ryan to see where Steve was. As I was rushing Moxie out of the hotel, I spotted him staring at Martha on the floor. I could only pray this was finally the moment where he realized what Martha truly was.

"We'll be there in ten minutes." I wanted to reassure Moxie, but she didn't respond, she only looked out the window with glazed eyes.

For the next ten minutes Renee and I sat in silence as Moxie continued to mumble softly to herself. I didn't want to do or say anything that would add to her trauma. I figured it was better to keep my mouth shut. I pulled up to the hospital entrance, and Renee hopped out of the back seat as soon as the car stopped.

"Go inside and tell one of the nurses she's in labor and that we will need a wheelchair," I said to Renee. She nodded and jogged into the hospital.

I reached for Moxie's hand. She clutched the fabric of her dress. "This is it," I said, trying to keep my tone light. "We're going to meet our little boy and little girl soon."

Her glazed eyes turned to me, but I couldn't get a good read of her emotions. We had just been through a lot and about to deliver our babies. I knew if it were me, I would have shit in my pants by now. "I'm very proud of you and love you so much. You're going to be an amazing mother and wife."

Finally, recognition came back into her face. "But we're

not married," she said in a sad voice.

I cupped her cheek. "Moxie, just because it didn't happen today doesn't mean that it isn't going to happen. We'll just have to wait a little longer. Besides, I don't need a piece of paper claiming that we're husband and wife. I already feel that way. Me, you, and Dillion are a family, and today we are adding two more people to that family. I am a very blessed man."

Tears formed in her eyes, and I glanced over her shoulder to see a hospital employee and Renee pushing a wheelchair to the car.

"They're going to take you in and get you registered while I go park that car. I'll be right behind you." I kissed the back of her hand.

"I love you," she whispered.

"I love you, too, sweetness. Now let's go have ourselves some Oompa Loompas."

The Pregnancy Guide

Month 9

Women

It's almost over. Thank fucking God.

Men

You didn't think you could be more in love. Both your partner and baby are perfect.

Twenty-four

Moxie

"Holy fucking, shit, fucker, whore face, ass licker, cow turd!" My deafening scream filled the busy emergency room.

"I guess she's starting to feel something," Renee said, looking at Miles with a distressed look on her face.

"Moxie, are you feeling pain?" Miles asked me as he

touched my arm like I was made of glass. I was currently clutching the sides of the sterile gurney. It felt like we have been waiting in the ER forever, even though in reality it wasn't that long. Maybe they were on the *Let's Fuck with Moxie Plan* and they figured if a baby head was not visible from my cooter, that I wasn't number one priority.

"Get away from me, you penis fucker. You and your stupid penis just had to enter my vagina and spit out its seed so it could procreate. That's all that men care about: spreading their stupid seed. This is not a garden people, you don't need to pollenate everything in sight."

"I'm going to take that answer as a solid yes," he said as he slinked away from the bed.

There was a firm knock on the door. I had been quite vocal and the hospital staff didn't want me upsetting other patients, so they put me in one of the labor and delivery rooms. Miles and Renee were both in the room with me, watching me intently. I think they were worried I was about to have some mental break down from what happened at the pseudo wedding. I tried to make sense of what had transpired today, but couldn't process anything because the contractions were increasing in intensity.

"Hello, I'm Dr. Newbauer. What seems to be going on?" A doctor with white hair and deep crow's feet entered the room.

"What does it fucking look like?" I snarled. "We're having a barnyard hoedown and were just about to square dance. You're right on time." I threw my head back onto the pillow, squeezed my eyes shut, and held my belly as another sharp pain echoed through me.

"You'll have to excuse her, doctor. It's been a traumatic day. I'm Miles Dane, her fiancé." Miles extended his hand to shake the doctor's.

"How far along is she?"

"Thirty-four weeks," Miles said. I heard the unease in his voice. Even though twins often came earlier than the actual due date, this was still earlier than expected. It was always the hope the mother could carry the pregnancy as long as she could so everything developed correctly. I thought I was going to hold out longer. Even though I was having small contractions here and there, I felt okay. The stress of earlier seemed to be enough to put me into labor. Maybe my children wanted to come out and kick Martha in the face to protect my honor.

"Let me examine her and see where she's at. Then we can make some decisions about what to do next. Have you already contacted her OBGYN?"

"Hello? I'm right here, assholes! And no, we contacted the mother ship, and they said they'll beam someone down to collect the alien spawn," I said, moaning and throwing my arm over my eyes.

"Yes, we called him on our way over," Miles said, correcting me.

I heard cabinets opening and gloves being put on. The last thing I wanted was for anyone to search my cooch. I preferred to lay in bed and pray that there were enough drugs in the hospital to alleviate some of the pain.

"Moxie, I'm going to lift up your gown. I need you to open your legs and let your knees fall to the sides," the doctor said.

"That's how I got into this mess in the first place. He told me to spread them." I groaned.

Miles chuckled and I shot imaginary daggers at him. He pressed his lips together and pretended to use a key to lock them shut. The doctor put some lubricant on his fingers and slipped them inside of me.

"Holy fuzzy shit balls," I screamed.

He withdrew his fingers and snapped the gloves off his hands. "She's about five centimeters. At this point I think we should proceed with the labor. Once your regular OBGYN comes in, he'll to tell you how to proceed further. Someone will be in soon to transfer you up to labor and delivery."

"Thanks," Miles said as the doctor walked left.

Renee looked down and me. "Moxie, you're going to have the babies today!"

"I want drugs. Someone get me some ecstasy or LSD so I can mentally remove myself from the situation." I moaned.

"You're in labor, sweetness, not at a rave," Miles said, coming up to the other side of the bed.

A few minutes later I was transported up to labor and delivery and wheeled into one of the birthing suites. I had to admit the place was pretty swanky for a hospital. The walls were painted robin's-egg blue and a wooden chair rail that wrapped around the room. Matching wood cabinets, which I assumed stored medical equipment, were on the furthest wall and a large bed sat in the middle of the room. A nurse helped me off the gurney and onto the bed, readjusting the fetal monitor that was placed around my stomach when I came into the hospital. We quickly heard the fast thumping heartbeats of the babies. The nurse wrapped a pulse monitor around my finger and another nurse came in to start an IV.

"Are you the nice lady with the drugs?" I asked her with pleading eyes.

"Sorry, sweetie, We're waiting for the doctor on the floor to decide if you will be able to have an epidural." The nurse tried to be as sweet and comforting as she could.

"Wait, what? There's a chance I might not get an epidural?" I started to shake and sweat dripped down my forehead. "I did not sign up for a natural birth! There is no way these babies are coming out of my vagina without me being numb from the waist down. I will cross my legs and hold them hostage in there until someone sticks a needle in me and clears the pathway for landing. Is that clear to everyone in the room?"

"Moxie, the doctor has to give approval for the epidural." Miles rubbed my arm.

"No! It will not go down this way. I came to terms about having children. I came to terms about my body may never look the same ever again. I even came to terms with my vagina looking like shaved roast beef after this is all said and done. I did not agree to having a natural birth. Go. Get. The. Fucking. Drugs."

The nurse glanced between Miles and Renee. She didn't know whether to get a doctor or a straitjacket. "Is she always like this?" The nurse asked Renee.

"Oh no, she's not. Moxie is pretty calm right now if you ask me." Renee grinned at the nurse.

The nurse widened her eyes and quickly finished putting the IV in. She rushed out of the room faster than I could blink. Miles took my hand in his own and gave it a little squeeze. I know I was being a pain in the ass, but I was scared shitless. My son and daughter were on their way, and I felt completely unprepared. What happened with Martha today was just more of a confirmation to me that I had no idea what motherhood meant. Throughout most of my life I only experienced negativity and anxiety when it came to the mother figure in my life. What's to say I wasn't going to pass that on to my own children. Even with the help of Dr. Gerber, I still carried that fear with me.

I closed my eyes.

"I can see the wheels spinning in your head."

"They're coming, Miles, and I'm not ready." My voice wobbled.

"Moxie, you'll never be ready. None of us ever are when children come into the picture. I was a wreck before Dillion came. I didn't have the experience you have with children so everything was so unknown. Even now, having Dillion doesn't mean I'm not scared about these two coming into our lives. You can't predict what's going to happen. All we can do is our best and try to lead them the best way we know how."

"I don't know how to be a mother. Look at my only example."

"There isn't an instructional manual for motherhood. Even though you didn't give birth to Dillion you still love him and protect him. You would do anything for him. I see it all the time. It doesn't matter that Martha was the one example you had in your life, you naturally know how to love others despite that. You fell in love with me, and you, Dillion, and I are a family. Soon we will be a family of five." Miles kissed my hand. In that moment I didn't need a white dress, flowers, or anyone telling me that we were husband and wife. Miles was all mine, heart and soul.

"It's like the show *Party of Five*," I said.

"Sort of. But I'm a lot hotter than Matthew Fox and you're a lot sexier then Lacey Chabert."

"Wasn't she the one who played the youngest child?" I asked

"Yeah."

"Ew, you're comparing me with a child! That's nasty."

Before Miles could respond, Ryan came running into the room. "Did we miss it? Are they here? Did you keep the placenta?"

"No, asshole, you didn't miss anything except Moxie

having a mental breakdown, which was somewhat humorous," Renee replied.

"Shithole, fuck face, mother puss bucket, testicular sucker!" I screamed.

"Oh my God, Moxie has Tourette's." Ryan covered his mouth with his hand.

"No, that would be a contraction," Miles said, pointing to the monitor printout.

I was starting to think my insides were going to explode. I watched a million episodes of *A Baby Story* on TLC and always thought the women on that show were such pussies. I figured labor was like having a bad period. But this was like period cramps times a billion. I swore to myself I was going to write each one of those women an apology note when this was over. I grabbed the railing of the bed and tried to remember my Lamaze. Why didn't I pay more attention instead of making fun of the fake baby's little testicles? The door to the room opened and Dr. Ford came in with one of the nurses. Even though I was in raging pain, I didn't miss the look Ryan and Dr. Ford gave each other when he walked in. I would have to remember to interrogate Ryan about—

"Oh fuck, shit! Get these demons out of me!

"You know I was on the eighteen hole, right?" Dr. Ford winked. Motherfucker. Did he not realize he shouldn't joke with a woman in labor unless he wanted hospital instruments shoved up his penis hole?

"Dr. Ford, I love you," I said through breaths. "But if you

joke around, you might end up losing your head when you bend down to check on me because my vagina might bite it off!"

His lips tightened in a barely contained smile. After he washed his hands, the nurse gave him a pair of gloves, and he sat down on the rolling chair in front of the bed. He pulled up the sheet covering me and proceeded with the internal exam. I tried my best to breathe through his dig in my travel tunnel. He removed his hand, stood up, and took off his gloves.

"When do I get the fucking epidural?" I clawed the sides of the bed.

"Do you want the good news or the bad news?"

"Dr. Ford, my stepmonster made my entire life hell, faked my father having cancer, ruined my wedding, and sucked out my soul. Give me the goddamned drugs!"

"Okay, I see we need to get straight to the point here. The good news is you're almost fully dilated."

"And the bad?"

"The time to get the epidural has past."

"Drugs, drugs, drugs. Heroin, crack, meth—I don't care, put it in the IV. I'll snort it if I have to." I tried to snort like a pig.

"How the hell is she almost fully dilated?" Ryan asked. "Doesn't labor take hours? I was planning on going to see a movie, then come back when the kids were all cute and cuddly."

Dr. Ford didn't look at Ryan to answer.

"All deliveries are different. Some can take hours or even days and some can be fast."

Oh, I definitely needed the details on... drugs!

"It's still pretty early for them to come. Will they be all right?" Miles asked.

"I've had babies come this early before and some even earlier. Right now their heart rates look good and things were progressing nicely at your last appointment. We will know more once they arrive," Dr. Ford said.

"No! They can't arrive. I don't want to feel my vagina exploding when they come out. Stuff them back in. Stuff. Them. Back. In," I cried.

"I'm going to get a few things taken care of first while the nurses get everything ready. Then we can start pushing. Okay?"

"No. It's not fucking okay. Do you know how much I pay in health insurance? This is why we are being screwed over by the healthcare system in this country. Because we pay a shitload of money into a program and doesn't offer you drugs when you need it. Fuck the government! I'm moving to Canada!"

My declaration fell on deaf ears and the commotion started around me. Cabinets were opened, sheets were changed, and people shuffled on different sides of the room. I saw nurses taking out sharp-looking instruments and putting them on a tray next to the bed. Pillows behind my head were being propped up and carts with body warmers for the babies were brought out. It all seemed like a dream. I tried to focus on what was happening, but I was blinded by the searing pain that was moving through my abdomen. Why were women the ones to go through pregnancy and the trial of delivery? Before I could make sense of anything, Miles was at the head of the bed with me, coaching me with comforting words and a cold washcloth to my head. Renee held one of my legs toward my body while Ryan held the other. Dr. Ford sat at the bottom. Everyone cheered me on as they told me to push.

I was tired. I couldn't do it anymore. Why should I try so hard when I knew I was doomed to fail? Tears streamed down my cheeks as I heard more faint calls to push. What happened if I couldn't love them enough, couldn't protect them? *Push.* Would I know what do to if they got hurt or had their hearts broken? *Push.* Would I be able to teach them to make their special mark in the world without screwing up their chances of doing it?

Push.

And then there it was. A cry that would change my life forever.

Twenty-five

Miles

3 months later...

I was in a deep sleep when I heard a noise coming from the baby monitor next to the bed. It started as a small whimper and quickly escalated into a gigantic cry. It was my little Sophie. I was getting pretty good at distinguishing the two babies. Sophie's cry was more like a long wail while Jaxson's cry was more like little hiccups. I rolled over to see what time it was: five thirty in the morning. It had been three months since the twins were born, and they were sleeping more and more through the night. I thanked God every day because going to work looking like one of the walking dead had started to get really old.

Jaxson came into the world first at five pounds five ounces. He had a little tuft of brown hair and, I would have to say, an impressive sized penis. I was extremely proud and may have shed a tear or two. Jaxson took on more of my personality, laid-back and low-keyed. Moxie definitely thought he took after me because he's constantly trying to reach down and play with himself as if his penis was a fun new toy. Sophie came roaring into the world ten minutes after her brother, weighing at exactly five pounds. She, like her mother, had red hair. Moxie insisted Sophie required a little bow to make her look like Pebbles from *The Flintstones*. As much as Jaxson took after me, Sophie took after her mother. If she didn't like something, she let everyone within a ten-block radius know about it. But that faded away when I cuddled her on a my chest. She fell fast asleep every time.

Moxie was exactly the mother I knew she'd be. She had a connection to the twins the minute they were born. When they put Jaxson on her chest after he came out, their eyes met, and the connection was instant. Every fear she had fell away and she became a mother. This was demonstrated almost immediately when Moxie tried to gnaw off the nurse's arm when she came to take Jaxson off Moxie's chest.

Moxie's relationship with Dillion grew closer than ever. He helped Moxie feed the twins and change their diapers— even instructing Moxie to cover Jaxson's junk unless she wanted a yellow shower. Dillion even read to them as Moxie rocked them to sleep. Granted, it was his favorite copy of *Moby Dick*, and it would sometimes make Moxie fall asleep, too.

Sophie's cries where getting louder, and I rolled over to only to see a mess of red hair covering Moxie's face. She was out cold and I wanted her to continue to sleep because today was going to be a big day. I got out of bed and put on my flannel pants and T-shirt. I crept out of the room and quietly walked into the nursery, hoping not to wake Jaxson. Although, I had to say… I was impressed he'd been able to sleep through his sister's demanding cries.

"Hello, sweetheart. What's got your diaper in a bunch?"

As soon as she saw me, she stopped crying and started kicking her feet in excitement. She even gave me a little smile that said, "*You're a sucker.*" She was right, I was the world's biggest sucker when it came to my kids, especially Sophie. I believed the words *Daddy's Princess* was going to be a staple phrase in our house.

I picked up Sophie from her crib and changed her diaper. This calmed her down further and her little eyelids started to flutter shut. I walked over to the glider and sat down, hoping to rock her to sleep. Like the princess she was, she went right back to sleep as she puckered her little pink lips. I put her back into her crib and quietly walked back into my room, praying her brother would stay asleep so I wouldn't have to do this again right away. I remembered when Dillion was born; having a newborn was rough. But having two was like trying to run a zoo with two constantly hungry, pooping tigers.

I snuck back into bed and closed my eyes, hoping that sleep would take me. But I knew I wasn't going to get that lucky. Moxie rolled over and pushed her locks away from her face.

"Did Sophie want you to change her diaper?" she asked in a sleepy voice.

"Yeah. That kid has an issue about being in a wet diaper."

"How would you feel if you had to sit in your own piss and shit?

"I would be a pig in shit," I teased.

"It's way too early for bad jokes." Moxie groaned.

I kissed her lips and cuddled her close to me. Within a few minutes Moxie was snoring lightly. As much as I wanted to follow her, I was just too excited. Today, I'd planned a huge surprise for Moxie.

When seven o'clock rolled around, I decided I'd stayed in bed long enough. Dillion would be up soon followed by his brother and sister. I would make everyone pancakes and get the twins' bottles ready. Moxie decided not to breastfeed, and I wasn't one to push the issue. My philosophy was that it's her body, her boobs, and I couldn't tell her what to do with them. Unless, of course, it was sex and I told her to push them together so I could fuck her breasts.

I was taking out the ingredients to make the pancakes when Moxie came into the kitchen holding Jaxson. She was so fucking beautiful and holding our son only made her light up the room ten times more.

"He was starting to whine, so I brought him down to have breakfast. He's like his mommy, if he doesn't eat on time there will be hell to pay." She put him into a bouncy seat and strapped him in.

"Is Sophie still sleeping?"

"Yes. It was so cute because she had her little thumb in her mouth, sucking away."

"That's going to be a tough habit to break when she gets older," I said.

"No, it won't." Moxie shook her head. "I have every intention of ripping off her thumbs if she won't quit. Thumbs are overrated anyhow."

I rolled my eyes and turned on the stove to make the pancakes. A few minutes later Dillion came wandering in. His floppy hair looked like it had been in a war and the opposing side won. I wanted to get it cut, but Moxie insisted it was part of his personality. I wasn't allowed to touch it unless she gave me clearance. Dillion pretty much agreed with anything Moxie said. That included nagging me about skipping a grade just because Moxie said he'd basically repeated kindergarten for the past two years.

"I heard Sophie talking." Dillion pulled a chair out from the kitchen table and sat down.

"She's three months old and already chatting away. She must take after her mother." I gave Moxie a wry smile, and she discretely flipped me the bird.

"I'll go get her. Dillion, can you hold Jaxson's bottle up while I get Sophie?"

"Yes!" Dillion shouted and ran over to Moxie to get the bottle.

Jaxson was all boy and even liked to eat sitting in his bouncy seat. It reminded me of some guy sitting in a recliner nursing a beer. I poured some pancake batter into the pan and sprinkled a few chocolate chips so they mixed into the batter. Moxie and Dillion loved chocolate chip pancakes, and today was a special day even if Moxie didn't know that yet.

"You ready for today, buddy?" I asked Dillion.

"Yes! I have been so good about keeping a secret, haven't I, Dad?"

"You sure have been. For that I will give you extra chocolate chips in your pancakes."

"Sweet!" Dillion said, pumping is arm up and down and trying not to spill the bottle.

"What's so sweet?" Moxie asked, carry our little girl into the kitchen.

"Dillion was just saying how the chocolate chips make the pancakes so sweet," I said, immediately turning back to face the stove so my smile wouldn't give me away.

Moxie put Sophie in her own bouncy seat next to her brother's. I passed the second bottle to Moxie and she held it up for Sophie while Dillion fed Jaxson.

"So what are we going to do today? It's a beautiful Saturday," Moxie asked.

It was time to put my plan into motion. "You're actually going out with Renee today."

Moxie raised one eyebrow. "I don't remember making plans with Renee for today. Oh my God, it's happening. I've got baby brain."

"You don't have baby brain. She wanted to surprise you and take you to the spa for a day of luxury," I said, trying to keep my own excitement in check.

Moxie's mouth hung open. "A day of pampering? For me?"

Tears welled up in her eyes. I became nervous she would be too afraid to leave the babies. "Sweetness, don't worry. I'm perfectly capable of taking care of the kids."

"It's not that," she squeaked, trying to hold back tears.

"Then what's wrong?"

"I wasn't able to see my feet in the final months of the pregnancy and I'm afraid I have snaggle toes. What are they going to think when I get a pedicure? They're going to be traumatized by my talons. I'm afraid I'm going to send them to therapy for PTSTD."

"What's PTSTD?" I asked.

"Posts Traumatic Snaggle Toe Disorder."

I laughed and put the finished pancakes on a plate and set it on the table.

"Don't laugh," she said. "This is a serious disorder that causes nail technicians to go into deep depressions. There's even a message board for people to swap their snaggle toe stories"

"I don't even want to know how you would know that, but I want you to eat because Renee will be here in about an hour and a half to take you."

"Are you sure you're okay with all of the kids?"

I walked over to her chair, bent down, and kissed her on the top of her head.

"Of course I'm sure." She had no clue how sure I was about the day ahead of us.

After our breakfast Moxie went to shower, and I got all the kids ready. I had a lot to get done before tonight, and thankfully Kelly and my parents, who were back in town, were going to watch the kids. I took out the list I had stashed away and looked over the tasks that still had to be done.

"Whatcha got there?" Moxie came back into the kitchen dressed for the day.

"Nothing, just some stuff I need to get done for work."

She eyed me suspiciously. "You don't write your work stuff on paper, it's all on your phone."

Before I could make up some lame excuse, there was a

knock at the door and Renee let herself in.

"Where are my beautiful goddaughter, godson, and favorite little Einstein?" she asked in a singsong voice.

"Aunt Renee, I told you. I'm more like Darwin than Einstein," Dillion said with his hands firmly placed on his hips.

"Of course! How did I possibly forget?" She gave him a crushing hug.

Dillion laughed and wrapped his arms around her in return.

"Glad you're here and remembered the little people in your life." I walked up to her to give her a hug. I whispered a thank-you in her ear and she responded by giving me a little nod.

"Are you ready to go get pampered, baby mama?" Renee asked Moxie as she went over to the twins and started playing with their little toes.

"Umm, I'm over here, you nasty ho."

"Sweetness, I don't think using Hostess bakery goods as an insult has the same effect."

Moxie was trying to curve her bad language around Dillion and the twins. I told her Dillion probably knew she was trying to refrain from swearing and the twins wouldn't know what the hell she was saying anyway. All the babies cared about was getting that formula filled cylinder thing.

"Okay, we're going to be pampered like the royalty we

are." Renee grabbed Moxie's hand and dragged her behind.

"You are a royal pain in the ass." Moxie groaned.

"I love you. Have fun!" I shouted. When the door shut behind them, I turned and smiled at Dillion. "Time to put our plan into action."

Twenty-Six

Moxie

"You look a little tired there," Renee said as she entered her car.

When I got into the car I pulled down visor and looked at myself in the mirror. I had dark bags under my eyes, my hair was a tangled mess, and still damp from my shower. It wasn't that I was purposely trying to look like Jabba the Hutt, but raising two newborns and an eight-year-old took its toll. I felt as if my days where like the movie *Groundhog Day*. Get up, feed the kids, change diapers, feed the kids, change diapers again, give the kids a bath because they puked on themselves, and go to bed. Rinse and repeat. I wouldn't give up my children for the world, but I had to say my days were becoming a little mundane.

"Listen, if you pumped out two babies from your cooch canoe and devoted your life to them 24-7, you wouldn't be walking around looking like Cinderella either."

"Oh you look like Cinderella all right. But it's more like the Cinderella who was covered in soot and a slave to her stepmother." Renee laughed.

I flipped her my middle finger. "I will remember this when it comes time for you to pop out little Indian and Caucasian children."

Renee rolled her eyes and shook her head.

Renee parked in front of the Vivo Salon and Day Spa. I couldn't remember the last time I was pampered. One of my co-workers had gotten me a prenatal message, and I was really excited to use it, but the twins objected to someone rubbing my stomach and kept kicking. I think it was because I kept telling them if anyone tried to *ooh* and *aah* over my stomach or touch it without asking, they could punch and kick to their heart's content. Needless to say, the massage was anything but relaxing.

A rail thin woman with short black hair greeted us when we entered the salon.

"May I help you, ladies?" she asked.

"Hi," Renee replied. "We have appointments under Miles Dane."

I gave Renee a quizzical look and she just returned it with a big smile. I found it odd that Miles had set up the appointments. Maybe he was trying to be sweet and sent Renee and I on a girls' day. Maybe this was a giant hint he thought I looked like a character from *The Living Dead*. Great, Miles thought I looked like a zombie.

"Miss Summers?" A large woman with a heavy Russian accent approached me.

I broke my zombie trance and turned to the woman. "Yes, that's me."

"My name is Olga and I will take care of you today." Oh shit, this woman was going to break my feet in half with her hands. They looked as big as cow hooves. I really hoped she didn't start mooing during my massage.

I knew that I needed some work done, but apparently so did everyone else. The salon brought in the big guns for my beauty overhaul. I took a deep breath and followed Olga to my first treatment—a mani-pedi. I prayed I didn't have any snaggle toes or Olga would have her work cut out for her.

A few hours later I had been transformed. Olga actually turned out to be a magician and gave me a manicure, pedicure, and a stellar massage. I even let her *trim the hedges* because I felt that after a day of being treated like a queen, I wanted Miles to visit my pussy playground. A man named Spencer tamed the wild beast and brought back my red mane of hair from the dead. It was about four o'clock when Renee and I walked out of the spa. I felt refreshed and excited to go home to show Miles the outcome of his special day for me.

As we drove, I noticed Renee wasn't heading back to my house, but instead got onto the tollway.

"Did they massage your head too hard?" I asked. "This isn't the way to my house, butt nugget."

"I know," she said.

I stared at her, but she just kept her eyes on the road.

"Where are we going? Are you kidnaping me? Are you taking me to a shitty neighborhood and leaving me there? I told you I was sorry for calling your mom a penis-sucking Vegas showgirl."

Renee laughed. "Just relax, you'll see."

Forty minutes later we were in the city and the sun was beginning to set over the Chicago skyline. Renee found some parking near a building that looked like it contained lofts. We got out of the car and I followed her as she walked into the building.

"Where are we?" I asked.

"This is a building," Renee said, not looking in my direction. I knew something was up because Renee couldn't look at me in the face without spilling a secret. She was a horrible liar.

"No shit, Sherlock. I know what a building is, but why are we at this particular building."

"Why are you asking so many questions?" She kept walking.

"Because maybe a serial killer is in there waiting for me when I'd rather be in my pj's relaxing on the couch."

"Moxie, for once in your life, shut your trap and just enjoy the moment."

"Whatever, whore," I grumbled.

"Slutbag," she said, but we both laughed at our endearments for each other.

The entryway was painted white and had modern furniture. There were several black and white photos lining the walls. I went up to one of them and instantly recognized the image. It was a picture of Dickie's, the bar where I met Miles. I walked over to another photo; it was a picture of the school I worked at. The other pictures contained a tent, "The Bean" at Millennium Park, Starbucks, and then a picture of the Art Institute.

It was a visual story of how Miles and I met and fell in love. Tears sprang to my eyes as I studied the pictures. My trip through memory lane was interrupted by a ding from the elevator.

"Ready?" Renee asked.

I didn't answer her. Something was up so I walked into the elevator and waited to see what was next.

"Are you going to tell me what is going on?"

"Nope," Renee answered, looking at the elevator doors.

"Is it a frat party with strapping young college guys dancing in nothing but their underwear?"

Renee giggled. "Nope, but now that you mentioned it, I kinda wish it was."

Once the doors opened, we stepped out and walked down a white hallway until we reached a door. Renee opened it, revealing a small stairwell which lead to what I guessed was the rooftop. I reached the top of the stairs and walked outside. The early evening warmed hit my skin and I looked at the tops of buildings that made up my favorite skyline which had a mixture of tall and short buildings. I could also see Lake Michigan sparkle in the distance. Then I focused on my immediate surroundings and was struck into silence. I slowly looked around. There were tables draped in white linen and set with stemware. Each table had centerpieces of blue and orange flowers. Twinkling lights strung across poles that were part of the rooftop, casting a heavenly glow. A few rows of white chairs sat around the chuppah. I wiped my wet cheeks when I realized what I was looking at. The chuppah I had made out of my mom's wedding dress was draped on top of four poles, creating the space where Miles and I would become husband and wife.

"Do you like it?" Miles's breath tickled my ear. I didn't even hear him come up the stairs behind me.

I turned to him. He was in black pants and a royal blue dress shirt with a white rose boutonnière. His hair was skillfully messy, which was the way I loved it most. He titled his head and a sparkle shone from his eyes as he waited for my reply.

"What is all this?" I asked already fully aware but still wanting to hear it from Miles.

"It's our wedding day." He gave me a shy smile and reached out to hold my hands. "Moxie, I love you with my whole heart and soul. Will you marry me tonight?"

"Is there a cake?" I winked. I couldn't resist being a smart ass even in the most romantic of times.

"Moist chocolate cake with raspberry filling and white buttercream frosting."

"Oh God, I love it when you talk dirty to me." I smiled, wrapped my arms around his neck, and brought him closer for a kiss. My tongue followed the curve of his full lips. He opened his mouth, letting my tongue intertwine with his. I pulled back, afraid that if I continued I was going to tackle him to the floor and rip his clothes off.

"Yes, Miles Dane. I will marry you tonight."

Miles gave me a quick smack on my ass. "Then you better hurry up, woman. Times a wastin'."

"There's a time limit?" I looked at Miles with a smirk.

"I only rented the space for the night. Plus, I turn into a gourd at midnight."

"Don't you mean a pumpkin?"

"No. I'm going with a gourd.

"Noted. Um, Miles, I don't have anything to wear. I know you have a thing for my yoga pants, but it's not what I imagined getting married in." I pointed to what I was wearing.

"Down the hallway Renee is waiting for you in one of the rooms. She has something you can change into."

I bounced on my heels with excitement and was ready to run down the hallway, but thought of a problem. "And what did you do with the twins and Dillion?"

"I sold them off so I could pay for this setup."

I put my hands on my hips and gave him my "I'm not assumed" face.

He rolled his eyes. "They're fine. Go to room 716 and get changed. People are going to be here soon."

Before I went back down the stairs, I wrapped myself around Miles and held him tight. "Thank you for all of this."

He kissed the top of my head. "I figured it was time we stopped living in sin."

I released him and smacked his arm. He chuckled and I left to go get ready. Before the night was over, I was going to become Mrs. Miles Dane.

Twenty-Seven

Moxie

I walked down the hallway to the apartment where Renee was waiting for me. I suspected she had some items for me to wear instead of the lovely pair of grungy sweatpants I had on. Maybe she had a *white* pair of sweatpants. I had to be honest, even though I had beautiful hair and freshly painted fingers and toes, I hadn't exactly felt that my body was back to where I wanted it since the twins were born. It's a little difficult knowing that Miles's impeccable penis was entering the same *hallway* the kids came out of. This was not from a lack of Miles trying to make me feel beautiful; he did that every day. But all I saw was sagging boobs, stretch marks, and a butt as big as Budapest.

I was aware women went through this period, unless they were a celebrity, had a professional trainer, a truckload of kale, and a nanny. I wished I was able to get the twins on the same feeding schedule, but when one ate and I finally settled back in bed, the other decided it was a good time to take a crap and whine about it. I was convinced they had a telepathic twin thing going on.

"How can we make Mommy lose her fucking mind?"

Yes, I was convinced my children swore, even in their baby heads.

Renee stood in the entrance of the apartment waiting for me. She was dressed in the same dress we had agreed on when we went bridesmaid dress shopping. She looked nothing less than stunning. The corners of my mouth stretched in a huge smile.

"You look like a high priced escort ready to nab a millionaire," I said, giving her a soft hug so I didn't wrinkle her dress.

"When I'm done with you, you'll look like Julia Roberts standing on the street waiting for Richard Gear to sweep you off your feet."

"You both look like whores." Ryan walked into the room, carrying a large white garment bag and a shopping bag.

Ryan was dressed in a black suit, a royal blue tie, and a blue daisy on his lapel. I thought Ryan was handsome, but he was drop dead gorgeous dressed up. He walked to the couch and carefully laid the bags down.

"Well, Cinderella, it's time to get ready for your ball." He unzipped the garment bag, pulled out the contents, and held it in front of him to display.

Tears welled in my eyes as I looked at the dress I had picked out the day we went to the bridal shop. The beautiful white satin made up the bodice and looked freshly pressed. The three quarter length lace sleeves held the dress on the hanger. The skirt was made of chiffon and swung around when Ryan took it out of the bag. The only thing that was different from the dress I tried on was the blue sash tied around the waist; it matched Renee's dress and Ryan's tie. I looked at my two best friends awestruck.

"How did you know what size to order the dress? I was pregnant when I tried it on."

"It took a little guess work, but the owner of the store worked with us. They also make the dress for non-maternity sizes. We decided to add the sash so it would hide that little extra baby love around the belly," Renee said.

"Baby love? I think it's more like a sign pointing to my belly that says, 'Little humans were here.' "

"Let's get it on and see just how skilled Renee and I are at getting this dress right?

I took off my clothes while Ryan covered his eyes. "Ryan,

you saw human life coming out of my vagina. I don't think there is anything worse you can look at on my body."

"I'm still having nightmares about it. I'll never look at cut tomatoes the same ever again."

"Gross!" Renee yelled.

"You didn't see it! It was like something from *Full Metal Jacket*. I just wanted to scream man down, man down!"

I rolled my eyes as Renee helped me take the dress off the hanger. Thank God, I had a decent pair of underwear on. Renee got a strapless bra for me out of the shopping bag. I was impressed she was able to get my bra size right, but she confessed that Miles looked in my underwear drawer.

I stepped into the dress. The moment of truth had come. Renee zipped the dress up my back, and I sucked in my gut as much as I could. Sure enough, Renee and Ryan worked magic; the dress fit! The three of us shouted with joy, and Renee tied the sash around my waist.

"There is one more thing Cinderella needs." Ryan took a shoe box out of the bag and opened it. I clapped my hands with excitement when I saw a pair of royal blue Converse Chucks.

"There is no way you can walk down that aisle without showing everyone how unique and special you truly are," Ryan said with tears in his eyes.

My own tears began and I crushed him and the box in a massive hug. I snaked out my arm and dragged Renee in our friendship lovefest. This day wouldn't be complete without my two best friends at my side. They were as much my family as Miles and the kids were.

There was a knock at the door. I rolled my eyes, thinking that it was Miles in a rush to get me down the aisle.

Renee went to the door and said, "You can't see the bride until she gets to the chuppah. It's bad luck, sorta, even though you already saw her."

"Renee, it's Steve. I need to speak with Moxie."

Renee's head whipped around to look at me. My eye's widened and my mouth fell open. I hadn't seen or spoken to my dad since the fake wedding disaster. I had a lot of anger toward him, not because of that particular day, but because he brought Martha into our lives. I had also thought a lot about what Dr. Gerber and I had discussed in our session about blaming my dad for not being there for me emotionally. I couldn't deal with that pain anymore, especially now that I needed all the support I could as a new mother.

Renee opened the door and my dad stood there looking… lost. He had dark bags under his eyes, and he had lost some weight because his clothes were a little baggy. My heart pounded. If Dad was here, then Martha might not be far behind.

"We'll leave you two to talk." Renee pulled Ryan with her out the door.

"Martha better not be anywhere near here. If she is I'll call the police and have her removed," I said in a strained voice.

"I left her, Moxie."

My brows raised. I had to admit I was surprised. Through all the hell Martha put me through growing up, Dad still stayed with her. He never got involved in the spats between Martha and me, probably chalking it up to mother and daughter drama. Looking at it now, I should have taken responsibility to really make him listen to what was happening between us.

He continued. "After what she did, I wouldn't let her back into the house. I didn't care where she went, just as long it wasn't near me. The next day I contacted my attorney and filed for divorce. She didn't go without a fight. She tried to convince me I was nothing without her and that you were an ungrateful brat."

He stopped for a moment and looked down at his feet. "For years I was so numb after your mom died, Moxie. She was the love of my life, and I missed her so much. You were only nine and I somehow convinced myself you needed a mother. I felt that you needed more than just me because I was so hollow and couldn't give you everything you needed."

Tears stung my eyes. Dad had never been so open with his feelings and part of me didn't know how to handle it. All I could do at the moment as listen to what he had to say.

"I was so blind to all the things she did to you over the years because I was so busy wallowing in my own grief. When you had the fallout with her last year about Miles and David, I felt you were already an adult and didn't want me involved. I didn't speak to her for a few days after that, but then she convinced me her intentions were good and out of love. I was so stupid. I should have opened my damned eyes."

I stared in disbelief at the broken man in front of me. Part of me wanted to scream at him that I was grieving, too. That I needed him, not a substitute mother.

"I needed you," I said quietly.

"I know you did. I just didn't know how to be there. How to be in the present."

I nodded, accepting his reasoning for the time being.

"This is my wedding day. I want to keep it as drama free as possible." I smiled a little.

"But I think that you and I both have a lot of healing to do and I think it's only going to happen over time. We can't just pretend that all those past years never happened. We both need to take responsibility of our actions. Dad, I know that while I have resentment over everything, I need to take responsibility for my actions as well. So, I'm willing to work on it if you are."

"Yes, I think that would be fantastic," he said, smiling.

"How did you know that we'd be here?" I asked

"Miles and I have been talking. He said you wouldn't be ready to talk to me yet and you were busy being the world's best mother." He let out a little laugh. "I knew you'd be a great mother, Moxie. You had all the qualities your own mother had."

"You mean she swore like a sailor and drank like a fish?" I let my lips curl in a watery smile.

"Oh, she definitely made her mark in the world. Even though it was too short."

He paused again, then stared straight at me. "I know it's a lot to ask, but I would be completely honored if you would let me walk you down the aisle."

I wanted to make this day special. It was the day I was finally marrying the love of my life. I thought about everything Dad said to me. We had a lot of work to do to fix our relationship, but the day wouldn't be complete without him escorting me down the aisle.

"Yes," I said in a small voice. "That would be great."

"You look so beautiful, Moxie. So much like your mother. She had the same red hair you have."

"I remember. I used to love playing with it, and I forced her to play pretend beauty shop with me. I also remember it falling out when she went through chemo." My voice started to shake from the memories of mom being sick.

"But you get your wit and stubbornness from me," Dad said.

My eyebrows quirked upward. "I don't remember you being so sarcastic."

"A lot of who I was went away with your mother, but I want that to change. I'm just sorry it took me this long and it took something horrible to happen for me to snap out of it."

"Well, it's nice to see you come out of your comatose state. Now let's put our shit aside for the time being so I can get married."

A large grin spread across his face, and he held out his arm for me to take. We walked down the hall toward Renee. She stood at the bottom of the rooftop stairs and shouted that we were ready to start to someone standing at the top. The loud din of voices coming from the rooftop quieted. Renee held two bouquets of the blue daisies and a mixture of orange flowers. She handed one to me and kept the other as we walked up the stairs.

We reached the top of the stairs and a piano started playing "Songbird" by Fleetwood Mac. A singer with the voice of an angel started singing the lyrics as Dad walked me down the aisle. My eyes were pinned to Miles. He stood under the chuppah, waiting for me to become his bride. He was dressed, like Ryan, in a dark suit with a royal blue tie. Next to him stood Ryan and Dillion. Dillion looked absolutely adorable in his own suit and blue tie. I couldn't help but look around wondering if the twins were here. Sure enough, Miles's parents were in the front row with Kelly, cradling my sleeping babies. Jaxson was in black pants and a cute little argyle sweater with different shades of blue, and Sophie was in a white dress with a royal blue bow in her red hair. The moment couldn't have been more wonderful.

Close friends and family surrounded us. This was how Miles and I wanted it to be. No giant guest list, no fancy hotel, and especially no cake with fake stairs and doves. Simple, classic, and very low-key. I reached the end of the aisle as the music came to a close. I turned to Dad and he gave me a kiss on the cheek.

He leaned toward me. "I'm so proud of you, Moxie.

You're a wonderful woman and now a mother. You deserve all the happiness that life has to offer."

"Thanks, Dad. And thank you for being here today."

"I'm happy to be here, too."

He placed my hand in Miles's. Even though Miles wasn't Jewish, we found a rabbi who agreed to perform our wedding. I wasn't the most religious person on earth, but tradition was still important to me.

"You look stunning." Miles grinned was so wide I thought his cheeks were going to explode.

"You're not looking too bad yourself. I might just have to rip that suit off you and—"

The rabbi cleared his throat before I could make a complete ass out of myself in front of everyone. Although, it certainly wouldn't have been the first time, or the last I'm sure. The rabbi started the ceremony, conducting all the prayers and saying all the things to make us husband and wife. When it came time to say our vows the rabbi looked at Miles and gave him a nod to continue. Oh my God, Miles had written something. I didn't know what I was going to do! I didn't have time to prepare anything.

"Moxie," Miles started, taking both of my hands in his. "Before you start panicking, I thought we could say some words from our hearts instead of traditional vows."

I nodded, relieved he didn't have anything planned out.

He continued. "From the moment we met, I knew my

world was never going to be the same. You had an instant hold on me and even marked me with the contents of your stomach."

Everyone in the audience laughed.

"You became the fire in my dark world, lighting it up again so I was able to see what my life could be and what I had been missing. Your love healed the parts of me that were broken, making me feel whole. But it wasn't just my life that you claimed, but also my son's. You became an instant friend to someone who needed guidance in a way that I was unable to provide. You helped protect him and nurtured him when things were rough. For that I will never be able to show you enough gratitude. I love your heart, your wit, and even your sarcasm because that's what makes up my Moxie. You are my sun, my moon, the daylight, and the starry night. You have given me two of life's greatest gifts in Jaxson and Sophie. Today, we cement becoming a family of five forever because we will never let you go."

By the time he was finished, I was afraid my eye makeup had been swept away in the rivulets of my tears. His words touched my core and would stay there forever. It was my turn to express what I felt about this man.

"Miles, you rotten bastard."

Miles barked out a laugh, along with everyone else.

"You pulled off one hell of a surprise today. However, even if you didn't plan this whole thing it wouldn't have mattered. I was yours since day one. There never, nor will there ever, be a person who fits so perfectly into my puzzle.

You saw me for who I was in the inside, past the sarcasm and the insecurities. You saw my heart and my soul. Your love lifts me up to be the best woman I can possibly be, and you make me feel like a partner in life instead of a leader or a follower. Thank you for bringing Dillion into my life. He is one of the most courageous people I know. I feel honored knowing Jaxson and Sophie are equally a part of you as they are me, and I hope they take after you because if they take after me, we're in for a shitload of trouble."

Everyone laughed again.

"To quote one of my favorite books that I read to the kids: *Guess How Much I Love You* 'I love you to the moon and back.' Except I might love you all the way to the dwarf planet formally known as Pluto." Dillion hollered with laughter at that last part.

We both laughed as the rabbi finished his part of the ceremony. At the end, we completed another Jewish tradition, Miles stomping on a glass. Then he pulled me in for a kiss that was less then appropriate for a crowd to witness. The air filled with mazel tovs and congratulations from our family and friends.

Twenty-eight

Miles

Champagne flowed, music played, food was consumed, and my balls ached. Seeing Moxie in that dress made me feel like a virgin kid hoping to get laid at the prom. I always thought Moxie looked beautiful, but today she looked magnificent. It wasn't just the dress, but the look on her face radiated happiness. We had healthy babies, a wonderful boy, and a terrific life ahead of us. I felt at peace… and *horny*.

"You look like you want to ravage her," Raj said deeply in his British accent.

I tore my eyes away from Moxie as she talked to Renee and their principal, Mrs. James.

"I hear she's married, but a freak in the sack." I winked at Raj and took a slip of my champagne.

"Does she have a friend?"

"Yeah, the brunette standing next to her, but I hear she's got fake teeth and a hairy bush."

Raj smacked my arm, spilling some of my champagne.

"Renee does not have a full bush, thank you. It's a nice landing strip."

"An invitation for you to land your airplane, no doubt."

"You're lucky you just got married, or I'd have to do something horrible."

"You already beat my ass in Scrabble, I don't think I can handle much more." We both chuckled, knowing that Raj was more brains then brawn.

"Just wait until we get to Monopoly. You'll be begging for mercy."

I excused myself from the conversation with Raj to get my girl for our first dance as husband and wife. I strolled over to Moxie who was now holding a fussy Sophie. Sophie was probably annoyed she had to wear that silly bow in her hair. To be honest, I'd be annoyed too, but my sister was adamant that she wear it. Aunt Kelly loved to spoil her niece and nephews.

"May I cut in? I would like to dance with my wife," I said to the women standing in front of me.

"I would be honored," Moxie kissed Sophie on the chubby cheek and passed her off to a very excited Mrs. James.

I walked Moxie over to the makeshift dance floor. The piano player and singer started playing "At Last" by Etta James. I held Moxie close in my arms and hummed in her ear. God, she smelled good. My little solider also took notice and rose the flag to half-staff. Since the twins were born, we hadn't had a chance to be fully intimate. Moxie had to wait six weeks for anything to happen down south, and frankly, between work and the lack of sleep we were tired. We were lucky if we weren't asleep by nine o'clock at night. That was going to change tonight.

"I have another surprise for you," I said, my mouth still by her ear.

"A chocolate fountain with marshmallows and strawberries?" she asked, pulling me away so she could look at my face.

"No. But we can involve chocolate if you want." I wiggled my eyebrows and smirked.

"Oh really?"

"Let's go around and say our good-byes so we can get started on our wedding night." I kissed her on the forehead.

She broke free of my arms. "Last one to the stairs is a rotten egg!" She sprinted to say good-bye to our guests.

We made the rounds to everyone. My parents had everything they needed to take care of the twins and Dillion for the night, and they were quick to remind me that it was a grandparent's greatest joy to be with their grandchildren. Earlier that evening, Moxie and I had made plans with her dad to come over and spend some time with his grandchildren next week. He beamed with excitement.

Moxie clutched Renee and Ryan, thanking them for being the world's best friends. All three had tears in their eyes. They were just as much part of our blood family. I peeled Moxie away from our friends, and we kissed and hugged Jaxson, Sophie, and Dillion. Moxie took way to long with her good-byes, so I picked her up, threw her over my shoulders, and carried her all the way to the elevator. I gave her ass a quick slap before setting her down on her feet.

"So where to, Mr. Dane?" Moxie asked as we entered the elevator.

"It's a surprise, Mrs. Dane."

"I like the sound of that." She curled her arms around my neck.

"What? That I have another surprise for you?"

"No, the part where you called me Mrs. Dane. I'm sure the students will have fun trying to rhyme that. Mrs. Pain, Train, Cane, Rain.

"I personally like Mrs. Insane." I chuckled as Moxie

swatted my arm.

I fended off her attack and crashed our lips in a searing kiss that quickly became fevered and needy. My cock stiffened and I drew my hand under Moxie's dress, grabbing her ass. The elevator finally reached the ground level, and I removed my hands from her ass and took her hand, leading to my car outside. During the ride I told Moxie how I'd planned the wedding surprise and the conversations I had with her dad.

"So, what kind of relationship do you think you'll have with your dad now that Martha is out of the picture?"

"I think it's going to take time. There is still a lot that we need to talk about. Maybe I could have a session with him and Dr. Gerber. I think there is a lot that she could help us come to terms with. I'm glad he's in my life and I certainly want him in the kids' lives. But I have years of pent up angst against Martha and I partially blame him."

I quickly looked at her and saw sadness in her eyes. "What do you think will become of Martha?"

Moxie let out a long sigh. "Most of me doesn't care what happens. But I still think there are unresolved issues. Last time I saw her was at the wedding and now I can barely remember what I said. I do remember smashing cake onto her."

Moxie was quiet after that and I could tell she was processing what happened with Martha and how it impacted our lives. We finally pulled up to the Four Seasons, Moxie's eyes lit up. She had always wanted to stay here, and what better time than our wedding night.

After checking in we took the elevator up to our room. I once again swept Moxie up in my arms and carried her over the threshold of the suite. When I placed her down she saw my other surprise.

"That's a tent. In the middle of the room," she said, pointing to the tent I had the hotel staff set up.

You could get anything done for the right price.

"Yes, it is," I replied.

"Um, why is there a tent?" She turned and looked at me, eyebrows raised.

"Because I got to touch you for the first time in a tent. That night I couldn't stay with you, and you thought I'd bailed on you."

It was a night that I never forgot. We were at a school camp out and I finally had Moxie alone in a tent. I gave her one hell of an orgasm and she prompting fell asleep. Dillion had a nightmare and I had to take him home in the middle of the night before I could say good-bye to Moxie.

"Yes, instead of waking next to you, I woke up to a Pepé Le Pew pissing on my leg."

I wrapped my arms around her waist. "I'm sorry about that."

"Oh I'm not, I caught the asshole and now I have a very nice skunk hat."

Laughing, I opened the zipper door and we both crawled

in. Inside, I had chocolate-covered strawberries and champagne.

"Wow, you went all out. It's like you want to get into my pants or something."

"Sweetness, I don't need strawberries and champagne. I'm your husband. That means I have a certificate for an all-access pass, whenever I want," I said with a sly smile.

"Is that so?" she asked, as if she were challenging me.

I crawled over to her and pressed my lips onto hers, pushing us both down on the soft bedding. We continued the rough kissing we'd started in the elevator. She pressed her hands on my chest, and I took them and stretched her arms above her head.

I broke the kiss, panting. "This time I will not leave you in this tent. I have every intention of making you come until you beg for more."

"You think to highly of your skills, Mr. Dane," she said as she licked her lips.

God, it was sexy as fuck when she called me *Mr. Dane* in her sultry voice. My dick was so hard I could have been one of the support poles for this tent.

"That sounds like a challenge, my sexy bride." I ground my hips in circles against her, lowering my head so I could run my tongue along her collarbone. She gasped and closed her eyes. I let go of her hands and traveled down her body and sat on my knees by her feet.

"Spread your legs for me, I want to see what's mine."

"Make me," she said and looked at me, her eyes hooded. She smirked.

Oh shit! I'm going to come right there. I had to adjust my hard-on straining against my pants. If I didn't get my dick in her soon there was going to be a mess everywhere in this tent.

Her knees were bent and I took each one in my hands, spreading them apart. I took the hem of Moxie's dress and lifted it until it rested on her stomach. She wore a pair of sexy white underwear that Renee must of bought for her. I had to remind myself to thank her later and then apologize because I ripped them of Moxie's body with a swoosh. Moxie moaned, her chest rose and fell with each labored breath she took.

"This pussy is mine." I kept my eyes on Moxie. "Forever. Mine to eat and mine to fuck." I was a breath away from taking her sex into my mouth, but I waited, knowing this sent Moxie into a tailspin.

"Miles, put your fucking mouth on me right now, or I will cut off your tongue and use it to get myself off!"

I bit my tongue to stop myself from laughing. Then I licked her from the bottom of her pussy to the top.

"Oh. My. God!" Moxie yelled.

I tasted her few times more times, and then I sucked her clit and held between my teeth like a vice.

"Fuck it, I'm going to come."

Moxie convulsed and I held her down with my hands. I was done teasing her and I buried my face into the sweetness of her pussy. It didn't take long after that for Moxie to come, screaming my name and grabbing my hair. It took a few minutes for the spasms to stop.

I crawled up her body and kissed her.

She broke the heated kiss, breathless. "Okay, I take back what I said. You have the best skills known to mankind."

I laughed and took her hand to help her get up. As the night wore on, we made love all over the suite. In the tent, on the desk, and there might have been a blowjob in the shower. We finally made it to bed and I held my bride close as I kissed her on her head next to her beautiful red locks.

"So now what?" She lifted her head to look up at me.

"What do you mean?"

"Everything has been such a whirlwind, from us meeting, dealing with the stepmother from hell, having kids, marriage... what's left?"

"Moxie, have you ever read a book that you really loved?"

"I don't read." She giggled. I gave her smack on the ass. "Yes, I have," she finally replied.

"When you read a book and fall in love with it, it always stays with you."

"I guess you're right," she said, snuggling back into me.

"So think of our life as a book; another story just waiting

to be told."

"I can't wait to read it. But only if it has a hot guy, good friends, and total debauchery."

Epilogue

Moxie

I had never known two human beings could produce this much shit. I changed Sophie's diaper and rocked her back to sleep. It was four in the morning and the rest of the house was sleeping, something I wished I was doing as well. But Sophie took it upon herself to make a crap in her diaper and wake me up from a peaceful sleep.

"I have a feeling that you are going to grow up and be trouble," I said to my daughter. Her eyelids fluttered shut.

"Well, someone has to follow my legacy." I smiled down

at what I have deemed as my mini me. She found her thumb and stuck in securely in her mouth, a habit I knew would be a pain in the ass to break.

"We are going to have a long conversation one day about sticking things in your mouth that shouldn't be in there until you turn thirty." I carried a sleeping Sophie back to her crib and settled her in. I made sure her blankie was near and nestled it close to her body. I walked over to Jaxson's crib to check on him. He was still out cold with his arms straight up and hands under his head. I loved when he did that. I told Miles it was Jaxson's frat boy blowjob look. Mile's laughed and said how proud he was for taking after his daddy.

I didn't feel tired enough yet to go back to sleep, so I walked over the dresser and pulled out the envelope I had safely put in there four months ago. I occasionally took the piece of paper out so I could read to the twins. I sat back down on the glider and unfolded it, looking at the words. It took a long time for me to put these words together. The night after the twins were born I was finally able to put it all together.

Dear Sophie and Jaxson,

Today, both of you made your way into the world with cries so loud I thought the entire hospital wing heard you. But it was at that moment I knew both of you were going to make your marks on the world. When I found out I was pregnant, I was petrified. I didn't think I had it in me to be a mother worthy of any child. I lost my own mother when I was nine, and the woman who raised me after that was cruel and vindictive. Feeling both of you grow inside me changed every perception that I had. With that feeling and the help of your father and older brother, I felt being a mother was something I might just be able to do. I can't promise we won't get mad at each other, and there will be times when I won't have an answer. But there is one thing that will always remain constant, and that is I love you, your father, and your brother with everything I am. So today, we all start our lives together.

To close out this letter I will quote Where the Wild Things Are.

"Let the royal rumpus begin."

With all my heart and soul,

Mommy

P.S. If all else fails, and I totally fucked up, there is money stashed away for you to use on therapy bills.

Acknowledgments

In 2013 I started writing *The Chronicles of Moxie*. I did it for fun, not thinking that anyone would actually or read it. It was simply a bucket list item that I would write a book. On May 19, 2014 I hit the publish button, thinking if ten people bought the book I'd be happy. Never, in a million years, did I think that Moxie would take off the way it did. The book exceeded every possible expectation I had and then some. People wrote to me saying how much they loved the book and when the second one was coming out. I laughed, thinking there was no way in hell I would be able to do it again. But I was wrong. Out of my crazy head came *First Comes Love*, a continuation of Chronicles.

I couldn't have done this without the support and love of those who surround me, especially my husband. He is my number one fan, my motivator, and book pimp. He is my 6'3 human anti-anxiety medication and partner in crime. Moo, I can't thank you enough. Thank you to my son who understood all the times mommy had to write instead of play. (Don't feel to bad for him. He had Xbox, and I'm sure that was way more exciting then mommy at times).

Thank you to the editing team at Write Divas. You all have the patience of saints for having to deal with my poor grammar skills, but hopefully it made you laugh in the process. Thanks to my street team, Moxie Minions, and all my other Facebook support team including beta readers and court jesters.

Thanks to my wonderful family for rooting me on. It

gives me joy to see my parents' face when I tell them about writing and how Moxie is going to one day take over the world.

A very large thank-you to the Moxie fans. If it weren't all of you, I wouldn't be continuing Moxie's story. All of the messages, emails, and comments about how much Moxie means to you warms my heart and makes me tear up. The fact that I was able to bring laughter into your lives instills a feeling I will never be able to describe. But for the meantime, I'll use the word *neat*.

And finally, to the sooty fawn-colored rabbit who weighed six pounds and had floppy ears. I named you Moxie twelve years ago. I hope you are looking down from that big carrot garden in the sky, proud of where your namesake has taken me.

About the Author

As a little girl it was always a dream for Z.B. Heller to become She-Ra Princess of Power. Since this dream was unobtainable, she spent what was probably way to long in college trying to "find herself". Becoming an artist scratched the creative itch until the stories in her head were getting to be to loud for her to get anything else accomplished. She lives in St. Louis with her husband, son and Flemish Giant rabbit Chloe. In her spare time she likes to read, stalk celebrities on Twitter and create the type of art that people scratch their heads about.

Other works by Z.B. Heller

The Chronicles of Moxie

www.ingramcontent.com/pod-product-compliance
Lightning Source LLC
Chambersburg PA
CBHW051413170626
46809CB00006B/2150